# FIVE MEN TO GO

Cliff Leatherwood rode into the ranch of his friend Manuel, only to find him dying and his granddaughter raped. Cliff made a vow to find the perpetrators and bring them to justice. His search led him to Sally Bevins, a bounty hunter also after the men and, joining forces, they followed their prey to Whit Fisher's range, the Bar F. Fisher was a powerful land baron, and two of the men Cliff had sworn to kill were his sons. The odds looked overwhelming, but Cliff vowed he would avenge his friends – or die in the attempt!

# FIVE MEN TO GO

*by*

## Stack Sutton

**Dales Large Print Books**
Long Preston, North Yorkshire,
BD23 4ND, England.

British Library Cataloguing in Publication Data.

Sutton, Stack
    Five men to go

       A catalogue record of this book is
       available from the British Library

       ISBN    1-85389-968-2 pbk

First published in Great Britain by Robert Hale Ltd., 1998

Copyright © 1998 by Stack Sutton

Cover illustration © Longaron by arrangement with Norma Editorial S. A.

Published in Large Print 2000 by arrangement with Robert Hale Ltd.

Dales Large Print is an imprint of Library Magna Books Ltd.

Printed and bound in Great Britain by
T.J. (International) Ltd., Cornwall, PL28 8RW

# 1

Mid-afternoon sunshine centred on the small of Cliff Leatherwood's back while the smell of dust and crushed rabbit brush swirled around him. The grass, brown and dry, swept south before him, and he could tell it had been a long time since rain. Far out to his left, cattle grazed, and beyond the cattle, the Hondo Mountains lifted jagged peaks against the sky.

Leatherwood pulled rein at a log bridge crossing a small creek. The Corazon brand was burned into a piece of pine posted by the bridge, and he wondered if the weathered post was the same one he'd helped Manuel Cardinales erect five years ago. Leatherwood felt a sudden shame for not returning for so long. He hadn't even written. But he and Manuel were like father and son. When they embraced in a few moments, it would be as though only a day had passed since their last meeting.

From his position about 150 yards out from the ranch, nothing seemed to have changed, except that Manuel had added another room to the main house. The gabled barn still set off to the left and an empty corral looped out from the back of it. He'd dug the well and hauled up the first bucket of water. It had been a way to repay part of what was owed; he'd never be able to repay the whole debt. He owed Manuel too much.

Leatherwood nudged the gelding into a trot as excitement kindled a glow in his stomach. He was anxious to reach the house, to see the surprise on Manuel's face when he recognized his visitor. Trooper, the gelding, had covered about fifty yards when Leatherwood's grey planter's hat went cartwheeling off his head as a rifle blasted over the distance.

He shouted, 'Manuel, it's Cliff,' but when

a second bullet whistled past his ear, he kicked the grey toward the barn's silvered outline.

He pulled in behind the north wall, dismounted with the reins trailing. He poked his face around the corner where splinters showered his cheeks as the rifle roared again. Drawing back out of sight, he considered this. In that one glance, he noted that the windows were shuttered, so someone was deliberately holed up in there. It couldn't be Manuel because his head would have gone cartwheeling, not his hat. Whoever was doing the shooting was shooting to kill, and Manuel could hit a nail's head as far out as he could see it. Was it possible Manuel had died? That someone else had taken over the ranch? If so, why throw down on a man without warning?

Leatherwood thrust a cigar between his teeth and chewed on it. He was a wide-chested man, with a lean middle and long legs. Two hundred pounds of ropehard muscle covered his six foot two-inch frame, and his blue eyes burned wickedly. He didn't relish being ambushed and he sure as hell meant to find out what had happened to Manuel.

'What's going on in there? I'm a friend.'

His answer was another batch of splinters flying off the barn as the rifle resounded over the yard.

Leatherwood ran a hand through his thick black hair. Damn it! That hat had cost him thirty-five dollars. He studied the square points of his stovepipe boots. He'd ride out of here. Circle around to the west, leave Trooper in a clump of brush, and belly in. He'd get his opportunity. It was only a matter of time. But, damn it, to have to crawl around in a white linen shirt and freshly washed broadcloth pants griped the hell out of him. Somebody had some explaining to do. And if that someone had harmed Manuel, all the explanations in the world wouldn't help.

He made a show of galloping Trooper out of the yard being sure to maintain a distance that eliminated any chance of being hit by that rifle. After heading north for about a half-mile, he wheeled west and circled in behind some rabbit brush fifty-sixty yards in behind the Corazon ranch house. He felt sure no one had seen him since a small depression formed a U-shaped gully leading in from a windmill. He had a good view of the ranch and noted again that all the windows were shuttered. He couldn't help wondering about that. It was early September and had to be hotter than hell in that house.

A faint breeze stirred up dust devils to the south. A brown towhee chattered off to the left as it sprang up out of its nest. Leatherwood took out his American horologe, snapped open the case. Quarter to four. At least two more hours of daylight. He considered the busty nude painted on the inside of the watch's cover. The artist had an eye for beauty. This gal was a winner. The kind a man always wanted to meet and never did. He closed the case and returned the watch to his vest pocket. His cigar's butt had been chewed to a pulp, so he opened his pocket knife, sliced off the pulp and returned the butt to his teeth.

His thoughts wandered to Manuel and he tried to push them away, but couldn't. Restlessness began to rowel his insides, leaving him irritable and jumpy. Patience was a virtue he had long ago developed, but he couldn't be patient about Manuel. That man was the only friend he had in the world, the only person he gave a damn about, and all he could do was sit here and chew on his cigar. Manuel's son, Juan, lived in New Mexico, but Juan was twenty years Leatherwood's senior. They hadn't kept in touch. If anything had happened, Juan couldn't have notified him if he'd wanted to. Juan had moved on soon after Leatherwood had become one of the family; he had never liked the circus business. With Leatherwood to take his place, there'd been nothing to hold him. If Manuel had died, the ranch would have gone to Juan, but he could have sold it and the buyer could have kept the brand. What! If! Why! Those questions couldn't be answered until he got down to that ranch house.

The afternoon droned on until finally the last faint glow of sunset shone redly beyond the horizon. Thin, grey light filtered across the land while lightblue shadows blobbed along the ground. Cliff Leatherwood wrapped the reins around his saddle horn, patted Trooper's neck, and said, 'Hold.' Trooper was well trained. He would stand here until he dropped unless he heard his master's signal. Leatherwood checked his Colt, the derringer strapped to his wrist, and yanked the Winchester from its boot. He crawled out of the thicket on his belly and elbowed forward Comanche-style.

His breath sawed raggedly by the time he reached the house. He wasn't used to this kind of exertion and sat against the west wall while his breathing slowed. He glanced down at the dirt and grass and sweat crusting his shirt front and cursed softly. In a country where most men took a bath once or twice a year, he had a fetish for cleanliness. He heard footsteps skip across the shack's flooring, caught the soft murmur of a woman's voice. Twilight fastened on the land as the shadows grew darker, deeper.

Leatherwood edged to his feet. He circled the house, but it was well constructed and all he could see was light gleaming through cracks under the shuttered windows. The talking and walking stopped; the only sound was a cricket's chirp. All he could do was hold until someone came outside, and the best place was the well. Sooner or later, whoever was in there would run out of water. It could mean an all night wait, but he'd have to tough it out. Rounding the back of the house, he made a crouching run to the well and settled in behind it. He congratulated himself on being smart enough to down some biscuits and tomatoes before easing in here. At least he wouldn't have to pass the night on an empty stomach. He figured that two people were shut up in that house, the woman and whoever she had talked to. He wondered who the hell they were, convinced that Manuel no longer occupied the place. Manuel hadn't noticed a woman since Josefina had died ten years ago.

A door creaked and lamplight beamed across the front porch. The door opened wider, and a slim figure in pants and loose shirt filled the threshold. She cradled a rifle over breasts. Brown or black hair tumbled around her shoulders, but he couldn't see her face. The woman half turned, said something to the person inside. The last grey lines of twilight streaked the sky. It would be pitch black in another ten minutes. The woman spoke again. Then she shoved the door wide open where more light could cover the porch and yard. Leather-wood scrunched down behind the well. He didn't know who they were, but he knew they were amateurs. She couldn't have made a better target in a shooting gallery.

The woman reached back inside for a bucket. Glancing over the yard, she walked cautiously toward the well. The cricket rasped again, and she jerked around so hard she almost dropped the bucket. She paused halfway between the well and the house, her gaze shooting out in all directions. After studying the barn, she quick-stepped forward until he heard metal bang wood when she placed the rifle against the well. The pulley creaked as she lowered the bucket.

He wanted to stand up so as not to frighten her. But what if she bolted for the door and someone covered her? He might not only lose her; he might get shot. He heard the creak of the handle cease; heard water slop over the bucket's edge and splash into the depths below. He pictured her hands lifting the heavy bucket and, at that instant, sprang from behind the well and grabbed her upper arms. Her scream shattered the night. She slammed the toe of her boot into his shin and, ducking her head, clamped her teeth into his arm. Pain hammered his shin bone, and it felt like she'd bitten his wrist in two. He released her left arm, slammed his fist into her bread-basket. As the wind whooshed out of her, her teeth loosened and he jerked his wrist free.

He spun her around so that her body was between him and the cabin. Wrapping his fist in the collar of the loose shirt, he held her erect and reached across the well to pick up her rifle. Her breath rode out in ragged gulps and he waited for her breathing to settle, realizing the blow to her stomach had left her nauseated. His shin bone ached and his wrist hurt like hell. He felt her shoulders stiffen as tension gripped her body. He rolled his fist a turn deeper into her shirt collar.

'Who else is in that cabin?'

'Only my grandfather.'

'Why didn't he light out here when you started hollering?'

'He's too weak. He's dying.'

15

He caught the soft, Spanish accent in her voice, noted the fear and sickness that made her tremble. For some reason he felt sorry he'd hit her so hard. She seemed close to vomiting. 'Why did you shoot at me earlier?'

'I thought you were one of them.'

'No, I'm not one of them.'

'I know that now. I don't recognize your voice.'

'Who are you anyway?'

'Carlita Cardinales.'

'Manuel's granddaughter?'

'Yes.'

He released her shirt and wheeled her around to him. 'Carlita, I'm Cliff Leatherwood.'

'*The* Cliff Leatherwood? My *abuelo's hijo?*'

'The one and only.'

'My God! I tried to kill you.'

'Good thing you can't shoot as straight as your grandfather.'

A sob caught in her throat. Her back was to the light and he could only see the round outline of her face. All her features remained in the shadows. 'If only you had come yesterday.'

'You said Manuel was dying. What happened?'

'Five men rode in. One of them shot him and they...' Her voice trailed off as her head dipped toward her chest.

He shoved the rifle into her hand, snatched up his Winchester. 'I'll carry the water. Let's get inside and see what can be done.'

He jerked up the bucket and, with water slopping over the sides, dashed for the house with her plaintive, 'Nothing can be done', reaching him. Dust spurted around his boots. Leather slapped wood as he vaulted the steps and flung over the porch into the house. A lamp sat on the table in the room's centre where its yellow flame cast a butter-like glow over the room. Leatherwood saw what looked like a pile of old clothes crumpled in the corner. A couple of chairs had been turned over. The room was oppressively hot and the spicy odour of cold chilli wrinkled his nostrils.

Carlita stood just behind him. 'He's over there.'

Leatherwood placed the bucket on the table, laid the Winchester next to it and, picking up the lamp, hiked for the rag-like heap. He dropped to one knee and lamplight sprayed over Manuel's sweaty white hair and ropy moustache. Leatherwood's gaze touched the blood-soaked shirt. A hole gaped just below the rib cage. He glanced up to Manuel's glazed, deep-socketed brown eyes.

'It's Cliff, Popacita.'

The brown eyes flickered, but no recognition dawned there. Leatherwood held the lamp higher so that it fully illuminated his face. The old man grunted. One blue-veined hand gripped Leatherwood's elbow. He was surprised at the strength in that hand, but Manuel had always been a tough old buzzard.

'It is you,' the red-frothed lips muttered. 'God is good.'

18

Leatherwood set the lamp on the floor. 'Carlita, open those windows. This place is like a furnace. Now, Popacita, I'm going to put you in a bed.'

Manuel shook his head. 'It's no use. We both know it. But help me sit up. I want to sit with my back against the wall. Then I want a glass of tequila and a cigar.'

Placing his hands under Manuel's armpits, Leatherwood lifted him gently into a sitting position. The old man's eyes closed against the pain. The muscles in his cheeks lost their slack as he gritted his teeth.

'Carlita, bring two glasses and the tequila.'

Footsteps scuffed up to Leatherwood's right shoulder. He glanced around for the bottle and glasses, and for the first time full light bathed Carlita's face. Seeing that battered visage rocked Leatherwood's self-control, but he managed to take the tequila and the glasses without blinking an eye. As he swung back to Manuel, the picture of her burst lips, her broken nose, her swollen eyes stayed with him while a scalding rage

19

flooded his abdomen. Again, his gaze flickered over the gaping hole in Manuel's belly, and he had to fight the madness that threatened him. With a steady hand he poured two drinks, handed a glass to Manuel. As the old Mexican gulped down the tequila, Leatherwood lit a cigar and stuck it between the old man's teeth.

'Who did this, *amigo*?'

Tequila dribbled from Manuel's lips. He puffed at the cigar. 'Five strangers rode in yesterday afternoon. They asked to water their horses. They were laughing and drinking, so I saw no reason for trouble. They offered to pay for supper, but I send no man away unfed. We sat at the table drinking and talking while Carlita cooked the chilli. Then, after they ate, it happened. One of them grabbed Carlita and threw her down on the table. I jumped for my rifle, but when I turned, they were waiting. I didn't get off a shot. I lay in the corner all night and listened to what they did to her.'

Leatherwood tilted his glass, felt the

tequila flame down his gullet. When those men had arrived, he had been twenty miles from here at Masters. He'd stopped for a drink, got into a poker game, and the cards had run so well he'd played until well after midnight. He could have been here. He could have stopped this.

'Cliff, I want you to find them.'

'I'll find them.'

'You must kill them slowly. I want them to suffer the way they made her suffer.'

'That's exactly how it will be. Now, tell me something: what did they look like? What kind of horses were they riding?'

Manuel coughed. Blood flowed freely from his mouth. 'Three *gringos*. A black man and a half-breed. I didn't notice the horses.'

Leatherwood gazed off without seeing. An odd collection, and one that wouldn't be too difficult to locate. People would remember a group such as the one who'd rampaged here. He would find them, and they would pay and pay and pay.

He heard the clink of broken glass, smelled the odour of burning cloth and glanced down to see where the cigar had fallen from Manuel's lips and singed a hole in his cotton shirt. Leatherwood picked up the cigar, beat out the sparks and crushed the butt under the heel of his boot. He hadn't cried since he was ten years old, but he wanted to cry now. Wanted to do something to release the terrible pressure knotting his chest. Manuel had been a father to him, a brother, a friend. The limp body lying there on the dirt floor was like a part of him.

Carlita squeezed his shoulder. 'At least he doesn't suffer now. That's something to be thankful for.'

He patted the small hand on his shoulder, picked up the lamp and the tequila and carried them to the table. She was the one who needed comfort; yet, she comforted him. He wouldn't forget that when he cornered the animals who'd done this. Now, he turned to her and, when she fell into his arms, held her gently. She didn't cry; she just rested against him as though too exhausted to stand. After a long time, she pulled back. 'You must be hungry.'

His gaze travelled over her face. Her lips were crushed and swollen. Her nose was a purple lump in the centre of her face. Her left eye had puffed so badly it was completely closed while a black bag hung under the red slit that was her right eye. Bruises covered her arms and he noted that the fingernails were torn on her right hand. It made him sick at the stomach to look at her. He poured half a glass of tequila and thrust it at her. 'Sit down and drink this. I'll be back after I bury him.'

'But I don't drink.'

'Drink it anyway.'

'There is a shovel and a lantern in the barn.'

He was tired and sweat-soaked by the time he had the grave covered. He called, 'Carlita', and she sleepwalked from the house carrying a small cross she'd fashioned from two sticks. He drove the cross into the ground. After she had murmured the Lord's Prayer, they trooped back to the house.

'When did you eat last?' he said.

'Last night.'

'You ought to get some food into you.'

'I can't eat.'

'You must be Juan's daughter.'

'I am.'

'What were you doing here with your grandfather?'

'My father is dead. I've been here for two years.'

'I thought Juan had three sons.'

'He does, but they are all married. Grandfather was alone so I came to live with him.'

'I'm sorry about your father.'

'He was a good man.'

'If he was Manuel's son, he couldn't have been anything else.'

A sudden breeze cooled the room. A coyote howled and the heady odour of dactura rode the night. Leatherwood's gaze shifted over the room. A deer head was mounted over the fireplace, two faded tintypes hung from the wall and a serape, a sheepskin coat, and a wide-brimmed sombrero dangled from a coat rack. The furniture consisted of the table, four chairs and a horse-hair sofa.

Finishing his coffee, Leatherwood reared back on the chair's hind legs. He hated what he was about to say, but it couldn't be helped. 'This is going to hurt, but I have to know everything that happened. Manuel tried to tell me, but I want your version.'

Water glittered in her slit of an eye and she swallowed painfully. Her lips trembled, and he put one big hand on top of hers re-assuringly. She swallowed again, took in a shuddering gulp of air.

'It was about dusk when they rode in. They wanted to water the horses, and Grandfather told me to fix them something to eat. We've never had any trouble before. They were loud and boisterous, but they didn't seem dangerous. Then, after they had eaten, they didn't leave. They sat at the table and drank while I cleared away the dishes. One of them grabbed my arm. He pulled me across the table and fell on top of me. I heard Grandfather yell. Then, I heard a shot and someone was laughing. After that, things are a sort of jumble.'

'When did they leave?'

'Early this morning.'

'And they were with you all the time?'

'At least one of them. They dragged me into the bedroom and kept me there.'

'When did you find out about Manuel?'

A drop of water wet the hand that covered hers. She seemed to have difficulty breathing. 'Only after they left.'

'Did they all...?'

She turned her misshapen visage to the left where she didn't have to look directly at him. 'I don't know. Everything was a blur. I can't remember.'

'Do you remember what they looked like?'

'Two of the *gringos* might have been brothers. They looked something alike, although one was heavier than the other one.'

'They didn't use any names?'

'No. And we didn't ask. You know the custom out here. I think one of the *gringos* was called Charlie.'

'That's not much.'

'Is it enough? Can you find them?'

His gaze dropped to her torn nails, the angry blotches on her arms. 'I'll find them. What direction did they take?'

'They rode west.'

He poured himself another cup of coffee. She still looked off to the left, her face, black and blue from hairline to chin, avoiding his gaze. He wished he could do something to kill the pain, but it was too late for cold compresses. In a way she reminded him of her grandfather. She hadn't mentioned pain, but her face had to hurt. She was all right inside though. Otherwise, she couldn't have tended Manuel all day and tried to drive Leatherwood off that afternoon. That bunch might have beaten her face out of shape, but they hadn't broken her spirit. The bruises would go away, but what happened would not be forgotten.

'Carlita, I want you to drink another glass of tequila and go to bed. You need rest.'

'I'm not sleepy.'

'The tequila will help. There's nothing to worry about. Tomorrow I'll take you into town. You can rest and decide if you want to keep the ranch. It would be a good idea to see a doctor.'

She sat quite still as he set a glass before her and half filled it with tequila. She put both hands on the glass and took a deep swallow before putting the glass back on the table. Her puffed-out mouth grimaced with distaste, and her slit of an eye studied him.

'My grandfather talked a lot about you. I am glad you are here for the end.'

'I should have been here yesterday. There would have been a different end.'

'Only one difference: you would be dead too. There were five of them.'

'For your grandfather and me, five would

have made it about even.'

'He was a good man.'

'Better than that; he was the kind of man every boy wants to be.'

She gagged on the tequila. 'He loved you very much.'

'No more than I loved him. I should never have left him.'

This time her hand covered his while understanding softened her brutalized features. 'Don't say that. You are a man. You have to live your own life.'

Lines formed from the base of his nostrils to the corners of his mouth as his eyes closed momentarily. Images formed in his brain, dissolved, to be followed by fresh images. Manuel had been as much a part of him as an arm or a leg.

Her voice penetrated his thoughts. '...between a Mexican and a *gringo*.'

He wiped his eyes. 'He was no Mexican and I was no gringo. We were men.'

'I meant nothing by what I said. It just seems strange. You must have been very young when you first met him.'

'Young and wild and headed for trouble.'

'Why did he take you in?'

'I don't know. I fought like a wildcat before he turned me inside out. Then he told me I could see the circus if I worked out the price of admission. When the circus left town, he took me with him. I helped put up the tent and take it down. I helped him set up his show. Your grandfather was the greatest trick-shot artist who ever lived. He taught me everything I know about guns. Your grandmother taught me everything I know about horses. They were wonderful people.'

'I never knew her,' Carlita's voice slurred.

Leatherwood stood up. 'Time for bed, young lady.' He helped her to the bedroom where he lit a lamp. 'I'm going out to the well and take a bath. There's nothing to be afraid of.'

He closed the door behind him and paused in the center of the living-room. Then he paced over to the corner where

Manuel had died, stared down at the bloodstained floor. Walking out to the back stoop, he filled the pan with water, found a bar of soap and a brush and scrubbed the bloodstained corner clean.

When he stepped into the yard, his gaze ran over the star-studded sky. Abruptly he remembered that Trooper waited out there, so he brought his little fingers to his lips and gave a short, piercing whistle. Hoofbeats ground across the night, and less than a minute later the big grey trotted up to him. He laid his head against the gelding's nose, stroked his neck. 'I forgot about you, old fellow. Come on. I'll get you fed and watered.' He swung toward the barn and the big grey followed him like a dog. Just inside the barn, he found a lantern, lit it and hung it from a nail.

The smell of hay tingled his nostrils as he removed the saddle and blanket from Trooper's back, stripped off the reins and led the gelding into a stall. He forked hay into the trough and brought a bucket of fresh water from the well. He knew he ought to brush the animal down, but he was too tired. The brushing would have to wait. He looked at the big grey's strong shoulders, broad chest, intelligent brown eyes. He understood that to most men in this country a horse was no more than a tool to be used up and replaced. Some men travelled with a string of three animals, rode one until it dropped, then transferred to the second one, then the third. But Josefina Cardinales, Manuel's bare-back riding wife, had taught him otherwise. A good, well-trained horse could be an extension of his master as well as a faithful, loyal companion. He'd bought Trooper as a colt, gentled him, taught him every trick known to the best circus horses. Trooper followed both hand and word signals. He would trample, kick and even bite on command. At the right word or gesture, he would literally tear man or beast to pieces.

Taking a towel and soap, Leatherwood ambled back to the well and hauled up a bucket of water. He found a board to stand on, stripped, lathered and dumped the water over himself for a rinse. Then he towelled down, jerked on his boots and strolled back to the barn where he found fresh clothing in his saddle-bags. He shaved, wiped the razor and, removing a bottle of bourbon from the saddle-bags, tramped to the front porch and slumped into a rocking chair.

The bath had refreshed him; he didn't like dirt and grime and would have been considered a dandy by many. He hadn't always been like this, but Josefina Cardinales had demanded clean hands, a clean face and clean fingernails at her table, and he had soon learned that to show up otherwise equalled the loss of a meal. She'd felt the same way about clothing. To put on a dirty shirt and trousers after taking a bath was a sign of stupidity that she would not tolerate. He brought the bottle to his mouth, let a long swallow glide down his throat. He squeezed his forehead fighting the loneliness. Two years after he'd joined the family, Josefina had died in childbirth, her child stillborn. Despite his grief, Manuel hadn't grown bitter. He'd been a humble, religious man willing to accept God's will. Leatherwood took another swig from the bottle. He didn't have Manuel's tolerance. He wanted to yell, to kick out, to break something. He couldn't cope with what had happened here last night. He wanted revenge. He meant for someone to suffer as Manuel had suffered. To feel the horror that still flickered in Carlita's slit of an eye. Feel it they would, because before he had finished this they would be on their knees begging. He took another long pull on the bottle, hoping that if he drank enough it would dull the pain that tore through his insides.

# 2

Shortly after noon, Whit Fisher led a band of six horsemen out of the Bar F. Unlike most men reared in cattle country, Whit rode tall in the saddle.

Whit's party splashed across the Rincon River. Thirty years ago he'd married a redheaded saloon girl, and they'd started the Bar F. They'd begun in a shack with a dozen mavericks. Now he lived in a two-storey brick house and owned more cattle than he could tally. The one thing that had spoiled it was Ruby's death. She'd never seen the boys grow, the Bar F gain its wealth and power. He glanced at Roy who rode at his left shoulder, wondering what had really happened on that trip on which he'd sent his boys. Roy's cheek had been ripped wide open. He swore it had happened in a fist fight, but it looked like fingernail marks to Whit.

Box Canyon loomed ahead; a cabin sat near the canyon's far wall. As Whit's crew drew near, three men on the porch strolled into the yard. Their leader seemed to be a 'breed, a man with a smiling, moon face and black, shoulder-length hair. Next to him stood a white man with a wide jaw and a narrow forehead. The third man was a black man dressed in a dirty flannel shirt, denims, and a brown hat with a Montana peak.

A flat taste filled Whit's mouth. He wasn't too impressed with this bunch, but they should be able to handle a few sheep herders.

'I'm Whit Fisher.'

'That's what we figured.' The 'breed's eyes flipped over Whit and his boys. He nodded at Bill, and his smile widened as his gaze settled slyly on Roy. 'Real bad boy you got there, Whit.'

'I prefer that my employees call me Mr Fisher.'

The 'breed glanced at his companions and, when he looked back at Whit, humour sparkled in his eyes. 'We'll call you anything you please as long as the cash is right.'

'I take it the other two take orders from you.'

'Up to a point.'

'What do you call yourselves?'

'Call me Breed. This is Charlie Reardon. He's Sam.'

'I guess Roy explained why you're here.'

'He worked around it, but we'd rather hear it from you.'

'I've had a few sheepmen crowd in on me. I want those flocks destroyed, but I don't want anyone hurt.'

'When you say no one is to get hurt, you may be asking for more than we can deliver.'

'You'll find one herder with each flock. I don't see one man giving any trouble to three men loaded down with knives and pistols.'

The 'breed put his hat on so that it sat perfectly level with the top of his eyebrows.

'Why don't we get on with it.'

'You're starting right now. I want it finished by tomorrow morning.'

'You pay now?'

'When the job's done. They're hard headed. You may have to use a little pressure.'

'As long as you pay, we stay.'

'Finish those sheep tonight. I'll have your money here tomorrow afternoon.'

The 'breed regarded his partners. 'We'll need one of your boys to point out the flocks.'

Roy nudged his palomino up to his father. 'I'll take them. I know where those flocks are located.'

'You go into Llano with me. Bill, you'll point out the flocks and help these men with the killing.'

'Pa, I'd rather not do this.'

'Do it anyway.'

'Pa, you know how I feel...'

'I know exactly how you feel. That's why you're going.'

Whit wheeled his horse and, with Roy trailing, rode through the canyon entrance out of sight of the cabin where he pulled rein. He put a studied gaze on his son. 'Roy, what's between you and that 'breed?'

'There ain't nothing between us.'

'He baited you back there, and it got to you.'

'Just talk, Pa.'

'Boy, you watch that 'breed. He's a mean one.'

'Pa, when are you going to understand I can take care of myself?'

Breed clipped up beside Bill Fisher. 'How much further?'

'About an hour.'

'Good. I'm anxious to get on with it.'

The miles faded beneath them. A flock of woollies came into view. After they circled the flock and descended upon the surprised herder, Breed and Charlie leaped from their horses and flipped ropes around him. The sheepdog was shaken by the incident. He growled hoarsely when Bill arrived. By then, the herder was tied up and Bill recognized young Gay Walker. Walker kept talking to the collie, and eventually the dog quietened and bounded over to its master.

Breed unlashed four heavy clubs from behind his saddle, handed them out. Then he turned and hit the closest sheep a crushing blow across the skull. The animal dropped without so much as a grunt, and Charlie and Sam joined Breed as his club continued to flail. The sound of wood splattering bone made sharp thumps. The smell of blood and wool coagulated in Bill's nostrils. He risked a glance at young Walker, saw the despair in the youngster's pale face.

Breed's yell jarred him. 'What the hell are you doing back there? Get out here and give us a hand.'

He faced Breed who stood in a circle of dead sheep. Breed's black eyes glared over the distance, and for once he wasn't smiling. Bill slipped from the mare and waded into the flock. The odour of wool and blood surrounded him as flies swarmed in. He bit into his lower lip, started swinging his club. He wouldn't be sick! He wouldn't be sick! But the pain spreading across his chest refused to listen to his brain. Every time he heard his club crunch against a bony skull, he felt acid drip into his stomach.

In a fog, he heard Sam say, 'That's the last of them', and heeled to see the black man drop his club, casually fill his pipe and light it.

'Let's find the next bunch,' Breed said.

'We can't leave him tied up like that,' Bill said.

Breed shrugged. 'If we untie him, he goes for help and that could mean trouble.'

'You untie his feet or I don't lead you to the next bunch.'

Sam's chuckle echoed softly as Charlie spat out a disgusted snort. But this was Breed's affair. Breed's black eyes drilled into Bill's blue ones. Then, moon face relaxing in a smile, he dropped from his stallion, cut the rope binding young Walker's feet.

41

'You're a fool, boy.'

They had an hour's ride to White's flock and spurred south without lost motion. Bill hadn't bothered removing his mask and thundered in on Tom White with the three of them.

When Sam whirled a loop and tossed it forward, Tom knocked it aside, caught the rope in his powerful hands, and jerked Sam from the saddle. Sam landed on his face. Tom yanked the rope from his fingers and lashed it back and forth like a bull-whip. The dog sprang at Breed, but he drew his pistol and shot the collie in the chest. He levelled his pistol on Tom. 'That's the end of it, young fellow.'

As Tom's hands fell to his sides, Sam struggled up out of the dirt. He grabbed his revolver and, taking two quick strides, hit Tom alongside the temple. Bill vaulted from the saddle to kneel by Tom.

'Did you have to do that?' he said.

Sam rammed his pistol into its holster. 'I've carried a white-man's scars on my back since I was fifteen years old. But no more. I'll kill the white man who touches me.'

Breed and Charlie moved into Bill's line of sight. They glanced at the body indifferently while Charlie fired up a cigar. Bill's head dipped. His fingernails made small, circular movements in the sand. It was just like at the old man's: things were getting out of hand.

Charlie grunted. 'Let's finish this.'

Bill heaved to his feet. 'There's a man lying there with a busted head. Don't you remember what the old man said?'

Breed slid over to the fire. 'Your old man wants us to hang a side of beef in the smoke house without killing a cow.'

Charlie took a last drag on the cigar. 'I'm headed into town. The old man will want to hear the bad news.'

# 3

Leatherwood guided Trooper into the livery stable's cool runway. The smell of hay and oats spiced the air, and the odour of fresh sawdust prickled his nostrils.

As he swung out of the saddle, he used his hat to beat the dust from his clothes and waited for his pupils to adjust to the darkness. A white-haired man in a thin cotton shirt and brown pants limped up the runway. The stable-hand dragged up a dipper of water from a tin pail. 'Hot day.'

'That it is.' Leatherwood scratched his stubble and waited for the man to finish his drink. Plucking a cigar from his vest pocket, Leatherwood lit up. He felt sweaty, dirty as he accepted the dipperful of water the stable-man extended. Leatherwood drained the dipper, swallowed a refill. 'I'm looking for five riders. Maybe you can help.'

'Maybe.'

Leatherwood's molars chomped down on the cigar while his patient blue eyes considered the stable-hand. If anybody knew who had ridden through a town, it would be the livery man. He knew horses and noticed them because everyone left his animal here for food and water. 'Five men. Three whites, one 'breed and a black man.'

'Saw 'em four or five days ago.'

'Which way did they ride?'

'South-east.'

Leatherwood removed his saddle-bags and bedroll, flung them over his shoulder. 'See that he gets a good rub down and plenty of oats.'

The livery man grunted, stuck a pipe in his mouth. He considered Leatherwood again as air made a sucking sound through his empty pipe. 'One of them's here now.'

Leatherwood's restrained features didn't move a muscle, but the cigar butt went to pieces under his teeth. 'Which one?'

'Calls hisself Charlie. Got a girlfriend over at The Corral. He rode in last night.'

After the stable-hand had led Trooper into a stall and began unsaddling him, Leatherwood heeled up the runway. His gaze found a blazed-faced black with the Corazon brand on his left shoulder. 'This Charlie's horse?'

'That's him. Fine-looking animal.'

Leatherwood teetered back and forth on his high heels. He scratched the black's forehead, a picture of Manuel forming in his brain. His parents, along with his two brothers and sister, had died of malaria when he was twelve. He'd been in a coma for ten days, but for some unexplained reason he'd licked the fever. He'd spent the next two years on a relative's Louisiana farm. His aunt and uncle had never shut up about the sacrifices they'd made to keep him, but he couldn't recall any sacrifices. All he remembered was the beatings and the work. At fourteen, he'd slipped from his room one midnight, stolen a horse and travelled west. For two years he'd bummed around – working when he had to, stealing when he could – and then he'd met Manuel and Josefina. They'd made him feel he was part of something. Now they were gone.

Slugging over the dusty street, he struck the boardwalk and followed it to the town's hotel. He crossed the lobby to the desk where a sallow-faced clerk swung the ledger around to him. When he signed, his gaze ran over the page to find a Charlie Reardon registered in room five. The clerk handed him the key to number eight, and he clumped upstairs noting Reardon's room as he passed it.

When he had bathed and shaved, he strapped on his wrist holster and slipped into a clean shirt and broadcloth pants. After wiping the dust from his gun and gunbelt, he checked the chambers, buckled the belt and swung up the hallway. He stopped at number five, knocked on the door, then knocked again.

He heard a giggle. A deep voice muttered

something he couldn't understand, and the woman giggled again. Leatherwood took a step backwards and slammed his boot into the door just above the lock. The door splintered and swung open.

A blond-haired man leapt from the bed as the woman jerked the sheet around her. The man balanced in a half crouch, his hands extended at his sides while his narrow forehead crimped with surprise. 'What the hell is this?'

Leatherwood's right hand rested on his Colt's handle. He saw Reardon's gunbelt hanging from the bed post, saw the man's clothes tossed carelessly into a chair. Behind him, footsteps pounded up the staircase. He threw a glance in that direction. 'Get back to the bar and tend to your own business,' he said, and slammed the splintered door shut with his boot. 'Get dressed, Charlie.'

The woman sat up in the bed holding the sheet in front of her bare shoulders. 'You can't come breaking into my room like this. Now get out of here.'

'Just concentrate on holding up that sheet, honey. I'll get out and soon. Charlie, I'm not going to tell you again. Either put your clothes on, or I'll march you down those stairs stark naked.'

Reardon lifted a hand reassuringly. 'Sure. Sure. I'm not going to give you any trouble. There's some kind of mistake here.'

By now Reardon had his pants and shirt on and struggled with his boots. Confusion marked his long face as he stood up and shoved his shirt into his pants.

'Rose, I'll be back in a few minutes. Just give me time to show this fellow he's made a mistake.'

When they halted outside the livery, a white-haired figure advanced from the runway to meet them. 'Saddle his horse and mine.'

Charlie Reardon smiled. He shrugged, spread his palms upward. 'What's this all about?'

'Can't you guess?'

For the first time a kind of understanding

49

crept into Reardon's gaunt features. 'Some-body set me up, didn't they? Look, I didn't kill that kid. Sam did.'

The stable-man brought out the horses, left them standing with their reins trailing and disappeared into the cool runway.

Reardon squared his shoulders; he shook his head. 'I ain't going nowhere.'

Leatherwood spat out the dead cigar butt and, taking one step forward, drove his fist into Reardon's solar plexus. Reardon grabbed his belly, doubling over. Leather-wood smashed a knee into his face and sent him sprawling in the dusty street.

Leatherwood tucked his thumbs in his belt. He watched Reardon writhe with pain, gave the man time to gulp some air into his lungs.

'Now, mount up and let's get moving.'

'Where to?'

'North. Into the desert.'

Reardon unsaddled the horses, then squatted on his blanket. He kept picking at his clothes, rocking back and forth, clearing his throat. 'I could use a smoke.'

'Light up.'

'I ain't got one.'

'Too bad.'

'How the hell did you know where to find me?'

'I kept asking.'

'You killed Breed and Sam? You been to Box Canyon? Listen, killing me isn't going to stop anything. The man you want is Whit Fisher. If it wasn't for those two boys of his, I wouldn't even be in this country.'

'What two boys?'

'Roy and Bill. They hired us to do the job.'

'Where do I find them?'

'The old man owns the Bar F. I've told you everything I know. How about letting me ride out?'

Leatherwood chuckled. 'We ride out together.'

They passed the night in restless sleep. At five the next afternoon Leatherwood called a halt. He took a long swig of water from his canteen, gave Reardon a flat-lidded stare. 'This is where you get off.'

Reardon's gaze shifted off to survey the wasteland surrounding them. 'You're going to leave me out here?'

'You called it.'

'But it's ninety miles from nowhere.'

'Yeah. It's a long walk back.'

Reardon wiped at his face. His eyes rolled in their sockets. 'You are crazy. I'll never make it back.'

'That's the general idea.'

Reardon's head lifted. His hands rose in supplication. 'Why don't you just shoot me?'

'That would be too easy. Remember several days ago when you and your friends rode into a little ranch asking for water? That old man died slowly, and the girl...'

Flinging himself forward on his knees, Reardon sobbed, 'I didn't touch that girl. Breed murdered that old man, not me.'

'You didn't stop it.'

'How could I stop it? There were four of

them. They'd have killed me.'

'Been a lot easier if they had.'

Reardon wrapped his arms around Leatherwood's legs; he pressed his face against his knee. 'I tell you I didn't do it! Give me a break. Please!'

Leatherwood placed the heel of his hand against Reardon's forehead and hurled him into the dirt. 'I'll give you the same break you gave them,' he said.

'Please! Please!'

Leatherwood lit a cigar, his gaze finding Reardon once more. Reardon's features looked like uncooked dough. Tears sparkled in his eyes while his throat contracted in slobbering moans. For a moment Leatherwood felt compassion for this thing that had been a man. Then he remembered Manuel's bloodied shirt and Carlita's misshapen face. He said, 'So long Charlie,' and nudged Trooper over to gather up the black's reins.

# 4

Leatherwood crossed the roadway and
entered the hotel. His clothing was stiff
from perspiration and the salt taste of alkali
crinkled his mouth. He asked for his key,
ordered a hot bath, and climbed the stairs to
his room. He tossed his hat in a chair and
shrugged out of his shirt and boots before
dragging a bottle from his saddle-bag. A
long drink washed the salt from his mouth.
The bathroom lay at the hall's end and he
found a tub of warm water waiting.

Back in his room, he lit the lamp and
swallowed another swig of bourbon. The
Bar F would be easy to locate and the Fisher
brothers would lead him to the 'breed and
the black man. In his mind he carried an
image of Manuel's pain-grooved face, the
deadness in Carlita's eyes. He could never

make the four of them suffer enough.

He locked his door and hiked up the hall to Reardon's room. Taking out his Barlow, he opened a blade and inserted it into the crack between the door and the doorjamb. He dug the knife blade into the lock, pushed the lock in, and swung open the door. He saw a lamp and a table off to the left of the bed. He closed the door, walked to the lamp and held a match to its wick.

A voice cracked from behind him. 'Now, goddamn it, let's see if you can touch the ceiling.'

His hands went straight up. Shock formed little knots across his shoulders. That voice belonged to a woman. He wondered if it was Rose and silently cursed himself for a fool.

'Turn around, but keep those hands reaching.'

He turned to his left, positioning his body so that the lamp would light up the direction from which the voice came.

'Well, I'll be a sonofabitch. You ain't Charlie Reardon.'

His gaze took in the square, solid figure so relaxed in the room's one chair. She looked forty or better with shoulder-length grey hair parted in the middle. Her teeth showed wide and yellow, and a plug of tobacco formed a lump in her right jaw. 'Who in the hell are you, and what do you think you're doing here?'

'I'm a friend of Charlie's. What are you doing here?'

She sucked at the tobacco, brown eyes direct and alert. 'Bull shit. You ain't no friend of Charlie's.'

'Name's Cliff Leatherwood. I just rode into town.'

'Bounty hunter?'

'I have been among other things.'

'Where's Charlie?'

'What's your interest in him?'

'Two hundred and fifty dollars. Same as yours.'

'Since we're obviously not friends of his, can I put my hands down?'

'Go ahead, but don't get any idea you can

pull that pistol quicker than I can pull this trigger.'

Leatherwood lowered his hands. He lit a cigar and waited patiently with his arms crossed over his chest. The woman stood up, but she kept the shotgun pointed at him. She was big-boned with no fat, and a Peacemaker and a bowie knife dangled from her belt. She looked rough and weathered and resembled a man more than a woman.

'I'd still like to know where Charlie's located, I'm getting goddamn tired of waiting around here.'

'You can quit waiting.'

'How the hell do you know so much about it?'

'He's out in the desert about ninety miles from either a horse or water.'

'Sonofabitch! You left him there?'

'That's a fact.'

She grimaced and the tobacco formed a bulge along her jawline.

'Goddamn it, I was counting on that money.'

He expelled a puff of smoke, shook his head. A female bounty hunter. Now he'd seen everything.

The shotgun tilted away from him. She scratched her cheek with blackened fingernails, then spat a wad of tobacco on the floor. 'Why in the hell did you have to stick your nose into this? What you got against Charlie?'

'Enough to want him dead.'

'Well, why didn't you turn him in for the money? He'd be just as dead.'

'I didn't know about the money. Not that it would have made any difference. I wanted him to have a long time to think about it before he died.'

'What did he do to you?'

'He killed a man and raped a woman.'

'He killed a lot of people, but that two hundred and fifty is a lot of money.'

He stared at her grimy face and dirty fingernails. She looked like someone who worked hard for a living. 'I can't place you as a bounty hunter.'

She wiped the back of one dirty hand over her mouth, and leaned the shotgun against the wall. 'Freighting's my business, sonny. I need a stake and Charlie was it.'

'Maybe you can luck on to another load.'

'Got any more of those smokes?'

He filched one from his vest pocket, tossed it to her. 'What makes Charlie worth two hundred and fifty dollars to you?' he said.

'He murdered two people in Texas.'

'He also killed a friend of mine.'

'You want to see him dead, don't you?'

'Not only him but four of his friends.'

'Well don't be so pig-headed. They'll be just as dead at the end of a rope.'

'They've got to know why they're dying.'

'Then tell the sonsofbitches.'

'What did you say your name was?'

'You can call me Sally.'

'I wish I could help you, Sally, but this is something I've got to finish myself.'

'You figure you're gonna walk up on Breed and Sam and take them? You need some backup.'

'Sorry. This is a one-man job.'

'All right, sonny. You just get your head blown off. When you get in a bind, don't forget I offered to throw in with you.'

Darkness still covered the land when Leatherwood left Benton the next morning. He was not by habit an early riser, but he wanted to put some distance between him and that hard-nosed old woman. Trooper tramped through damp, brown-grass country that would leave tracks, but as soon as the sun rose it would dry and the trodden patches would spring up like the grass in surrounding areas.

At dusk he pulled rein, unsaddled the gelding, fed and watered him. There was no need for hobbles. Trooper was too well trained. A band of coyotes couldn't scare him off. Leatherwood ate cold chow washed down with three cups of hot coffee. Then he threw out his bedroll, arranged his saddle for a pillow and, after lighting a cigar, sat cross-legged on his blankets.

He located a bottle of bourbon in one of his saddle-bags and sipped from the bottle. About threequarters of a mile out, the orange glow of a campfire flickered. It had to be Sally's. She might be a woman, but damn if there was anything womanly about her. She was as tough as a Texas cactus.

Daylight found him approaching the mountains. He didn't bother to look back because he knew someone probably joggled after him. He'd bet a pair of boots that someone was Sally. He held Trooper at a steady lope, a pace the big gelding could keep all day, and watched the grass edge from pale to rich green. About noon, he spotted a shack and obliqued that way. He needed some fresh water.

Trooper's hoofbeats brought a thin man into the yard followed by a yellow-headed girl wearing a faded sunbonnet. Leather-wood reined up by the man who positioned himself by the well. 'Mind if I fill my canteen and water my horse?'

'Help yourself.'

Leatherwood stepped from the gelding. He opened his canteen and poured out tepid water. Dropping the bucket into the well, he hauled up fresh water and filled his canteen. 'How far is it to Llano?'

'About ten hours. Been riding long?'

'A few days. I got business in Llano with someone called Fisher.'

'Whit Fisher. He owns the Bar F and about everything else in that country.'

'I met his boys in Benton some weeks ago. The old man anything like them?'

'A lot like Roy, but he's tougher and straighter.'

'How far is the Bar F from here?'

'Four or five hour ride. It's a lot closer than Llano. Maybe you ought to ride into the ranch and save yourself some travelling.'

When he rode out of the yard, the afternoon sun cast short shadows, and the land shimmered for long distances. This was cattle country with lush, green grass sweeping away in all directions. He spotted a line of cottonwoods far to his right and assumed they followed the river. Far ahead he saw what appeared to be a group of horsemen. A hawk winged overhead, its shadow swooping gracefully over the land. Some time later he found a waterhole where he smoked a cigar and enjoyed the solitude while Trooper rested. Mounting the grey, he took one backward look to focus on the lone figure in the distance. She could dog him, but when the time came, he would shake her.

# 5

Night found him at an empty line camp with fresh water and good grass. He'd eaten his supper and finished his second cup of coffee when he heard hoofbeats.

'It's me.'

Minutes later, Sally walked a white-faced mule into camp. Her brown eyes looked black under her downturned hat brim, and little lines of fatigue spread out from the corner of her lips.

'Anything in that coffee pot?' When Leatherwood nodded, she plucked a tin cup from her saddle-bag, poured herself some java, and squatted off to his left.

'What are you going to do when you catch those two sonsabitches?'

'Haven't figured it out yet.'

She tossed down the coffee, set the cup on

the ground, and fished a length of Twist from her pocket. She bit off a chunk before ramming the Twist back into her pocket. Leaning back on her arms, she crossed her legs at the ankles and surveyed the skyline. 'You sure look duded up considering you been on the trail two days.'

'That windmill came in handy. I had a bath.'

'A bath! Well I'll be a sonofabitch.'

'You got something against bathing?'

'Not if I need to.'

'You need to now.'

Sally spat a slug of tobacco juice, shook her head. 'Goddamn, but I sure had you pegged wrong. If you think some toilet-smelling sissy is gonna take Breed and Sam, you got another think coming.' Sally shoved her hat forward, scratched the back of her head. 'I remember once when I was mule-skinning for the army. We'd been on the trail about a week, hotter than hell let me tell you, when we came across this creek. That water looked so cool we just shucked our clothes and dove in. About that time, this sonofabitch major rode by. Seen me splashing around out there with the men and like to have had a goddamn fit. Fired me on the spot. Been against baths ever since.'

'You think you're pretty tough don't you?'

'Tough enough, sonny.'

'You come between me, Breed and Sam, you may have a chance to prove it.'

She gummed the tobacco around in her mouth while her brown eyes considered him. She was solid of shoulder, big of bone. A smile played around her mouth. 'Listen sonny, you may be glad to have me around before this is over.'

'Don't count on it.'

'You can't take both those sonsabitches at the same time.'

'Then I'll have to figure out a way to take them one at a time.'

'What if they know you're after them?'

'There's only one way they can know that.'

'Well, goddamn it, don't you bet your life I'm above it.'

He made a lightning move that lined his revolver straight at her. His blue eyes smoked over the distance and the contours of his face lay hard and firm.

She spat out a slug of tobacco. 'You ain't going to shoot me. You ain't got it in you.'

'You're right. I ain't going to shoot you. But I could sure blow the head off that mule of yours. That might slow you down a bit.'

For the first time she didn't seem so cocksure. Her brown eyes blinked, and her shoulders made a conciliatory gesture under the flannel shirt. 'Goddamn! It would hurt like hell if you did anything to Nellie. We've been together a long time. Why are you so set on killing those sonsabitches? I can't understand why it makes any difference how they die, as long as they die.'

'Like I told you. They wronged some people.'

Sally's lips pursed as she spat out another stream of tobacco juice. 'You're fast. Maybe as fast as Breed, but I still say you could use some help.'

'A man mends his own fences. That way he don't have to feel obliged.'

Sally gummed the tobacco around in her mouth, shook her head. 'You're a real loner, ain't you?'

Leatherwood glanced at the fire. His lips thinned as his thoughts shot back to Manuel. He was alone all right. If only he hadn't got into that poker game. If only he'd been at Manuel's. But all the ifs in the world wouldn't change things. All he could do now was make those bastards pay. Remembering how Charlie had begged, how his face had turned pasty white when he'd realized he was going to die, helped a little. Watching disbelief and terror blur the features of the others would help more, although nothing would fill the void that Manuel's death had created.

Sally flipped off her wide-brimmed hat, scratched behind her ear. Her brown eyes studied him across the fire and her face grew pensive. 'I think I know what those people meant to you, sonny, but killing ain't gonna bring them back.'

'Anybody who says revenge don't pay has never been there.'

'No need in talking to a hard head like you. Let's get some sleep.'

When he awoke, dawn's pink fingers brushed the sky. Sally had a fire going and the smell of hot coffee and bacon filled the air.

'Here's your breakfast, sonny. Got to look out for my partner.'

'Now that's nice. There ain't nobody else too worried about old Cliff.'

At noon they stopped to stretch and eat a cold meal. They rode out without a word passing between them. Sally sucked on a chunk of Twist while Leatherwood smoked his second cigar.

About two o'clock, a cabin's weathered siding gleamed ahead, whereupon Sally said, 'Why don't we get some fresh water?'

An unfinished barn rose off to the left and a well stood between the barn and the house. As they trotted into the yard, a 'Hold it right there', bellowed out from the unpainted shack. A man with a shotgun eased through the doorway. He was squat and solid with wide shoulders and a bull-like neck.

'What the hell are you two doing on my land?'

'Needed some fresh water,' Sally replied.

'Find your water elsewhere.'

Sally sucked at the tobacco plug. Her face pursed strangely. 'Goddamn! Amos White, is that you?'

The squat man's blue eyes widened; then, a grin spread over his stolid features. The shotgun's muzzle pointed groundward as he rushed out towards them. 'Sally! Sally Bevins. Well, I'll be an old horsethief. What are you doing in these parts?'

Sally swung off the mule and pumped the man's hand. 'Just riding through. Sure didn't expect to find you here. Thought you was still in the freight business.

'I'm running sheep.' His gaze swept over

Leatherwood, took in his gun and holster. 'Who's he?'

'My partner, Cliff Leatherwood.'

Amos stuck out his hand. 'Glad to know you. Don't mean to act unfriendly, but with the kind of trouble I've been having I don't trust nobody.'

Sally's left hand rested on the hilt of her bowie knife. 'How's Jennie?'

'She's fine.' Amos cupped his hand to his mouth. 'Jennie, come here. Bring the kids.'

Leatherwood lit a cigar as a woman in her early forties stepped from the house followed by a boy and a girl. The woman was heavy-set like her husband, with long red hair pinned up by a horn comb. The lines in her cheeks faded a little when she recognized Sally. As they embraced, Leatherwood noted her work-worn hands and broken fingernails.

Sally pulled back and her brown eyes rested on the children. 'John and Karen. Guess you don't even remember me. Where's Tom?'

71

All the happiness seeped out of Amos's broad countenance. 'Tom was murdered about a week ago.'

Sally's jawline lengthened. 'Well I'll be... You did say *murdered?*'

'That's what I said.'

'Did the law catch who done it?'

Amos snorted disgustedly. 'Whatever law there is around here belongs to Whit Fisher.'

'Why'd it happen?'

'Whit and his men raided my flock. I guess they killed Tom so he couldn't identify them.'

Jennie smoothed the back of her hair. 'Why don't you two come inside. I'll make some coffee.'

'Sure thing,' Sally said. She glanced up at Leatherwood. 'You know, you ain't had a bath today.'

Leatherwood shrugged and swung down from the grey. He might learn a great deal from the Whites. They could fill him in on Fisher and the rest of the country. If he could get Amos off to one side, he could find out where Box Canyon was located plus what Amos might know about Breed and Sam.

Amos told his son to take the horse into the barn and then led the way into the small but clean cabin. The furniture consisted of some horsehair chairs and a wooden rocker. The bedroom was off to one side, and through an open doorway Leatherwood saw an iron stove and part of a table. It was evident these folks didn't own much in the way of worldly possessions.

As Jennie went back into the kitchen, Cliff Leatherwood and the others sat down. He noted that the house was well constructed which meant that Amos was pretty handy.

Sally crossed her legs and took off her hat. Amos had lowered his solid bulk in the rocker. He had a wide, stubborn face with the kind of skin that always looked sunburned. His big powerful hands gripped his red suspenders as slowly he rocked back and forth.

Sally grunted, 'Never expected to run into

you out here.'

'Jennie figured it was time to stop working for the other fellow. We decided to get our own place.'

Jennie walked in from the kitchen. 'This is all my doing. Amos didn't want to leave freighting.'

'Don't go blaming yourself,' Amos said. 'Things happen.'

Jennie bared her teeth, glanced down at her hands. 'Maybe you can talk some sense into him, Sally. I think we ought to leave before someone else gets killed.'

Amos's pink countenance reddened. 'Everything we own is tied up in this place. Fisher ain't gonna run me off. God forgive me, I'd like to kill that bastard.'

A faraway look came to Jennie's eyes. 'That wouldn't bring Tom back.'

'It would make me sleep a hell of a lot better.'

'We still have John and Karen. We could pull stakes and start some place else. This place ain't worth it.'

Amos banged one heavy fist on the rocker arm. 'Maybe before it wasn't, but my son's blood is in this ground.'

Leatherwood blew out a streamer of smoke. 'How many riders has this Fisher got?'

'Twenty, twenty-five. More at round-up.'

'How many men backing you?'

'There's just the four of us.'

'Don't seem like much of a show. I'd say your wife is right.'

Amos's blue eyes shaded to a winter grey. 'Mister, I don't know you, but if Sally says you're all right, then you're all right. But I don't give a damn what you think. This is my land. Nobody's gonna send me packing.'

Jennie edged over to the rocker. She put her arms around her husband's head, pressed it into her stomach. 'Amos White, you're a fool. If anything happens to you, what about the children?'

'Nothing's gonna happen to me. Now bring the coffee.'

The meal consisted of mutton, beans, bread and black coffee. Amos passed the tray of mutton to Leatherwood. 'We're low on grub. They won't sell to us in Llano any more. Guess we'll have to do our buying at Hookerville.'

'That's a two-day ride,' Sally muttered.

'It's not too convenient. Karen, you and John stop that. You don't bicker at the table.'

Leatherwood spread butter on a steaming biscuit. Fisher knew how to play his cards; if he couldn't run the sheepmen out, he'd starve them out.

Sally sliced off a chunk of mutton, dipped up some beans. 'That goddamned store-keeper don't know me. I could drive the wagon in and bring out a load of supplies.'

Amos shook his head. 'It won't work. He knows the wagon.'

Sally's teeth flashed as she cut off a bite of bread. 'Maybe I could convince him he was wrong about the wagon. I never knew a store-keeper yet who had a backbone.'

'It's not the store-keeper, it's Whit Fisher.

No, Sally. I won't have you fighting the Bar F because of me.'

'Why Amos White, as much as you've...'

Glass splintered across the room. A rifle blasted and splinters flew off the mantel as another gunshot split the night. Leather-wood leaped to his feet. He blew out the lamp. 'Hit the floor everybody and stay there.' Bullets whined overhead as more gunfire enlivened the surroundings. Leatherwood heard John say, 'Mamma', caught Jennie's, 'It's all right, John. Now, Karen, stop that sniffling.' A slug struck the iron stove, ricocheted through the living-room. Amos gritted. 'Those dirty bastards', while Sally muttered, 'My shotgun's in the corner. I'll get it and give those sonsabitches some of their own medicine.'

'Stay where you are. They're not trying to hit anybody. Someone would be dead if they were.'

'You mean you want to lie here and take it?'

'We haven't got any choice. Besides,

they're playing a game. It'll be over soon.'

'It's a hell of a game.'

Bullets ripped through the small house for another ten minutes while the six of them huddled on the floor. Then someone let out a yell as hoofbeats pounded into the night.

Leatherwood crawled to his feet, struck a match. 'It's over for now. They won't be back.'

# 6

After breakfast the next morning, Leatherwood stood on the front porch and lit his
first cigar. The night had been hectic. It had
been difficult to calm the kids and Sally and
Amos had wanted to go after the raiding
party. But Leatherwood had pointed out
that they couldn't track the raiders in the
dark.

Sally and Amos shuffled out on the porch
whereupon Sally bit off a hunk of Twist and
handed a plug to Amos. 'I reckon you two
will be headed for Llano,' Amos said.

'I reckon,' Leatherwood grunted.

Far out he sighted a band of riders.
Hoofbeats strengthened as the horsemen
neared. Leatherwood counted eight riders.
His teeth closed on the cigar as he slipped
his thumbs through his belt loops.

Sally shot a stream of spittle into the yard. 'Cliff, you thinking what I'm thinking?'

'It's the same ones all right.'

'We'll give those sonsabitches all they want this morning. Come on, Amos, let's grab those shotguns.'

Leatherwood heard footsteps: the door opened and closed. Amos said, 'Jennie, you keep John and Karen in here.' Then the door opened and closed again.

The horsemen neared the yard. Their leader, on a palomino, closely followed by a young fellow on a reddish mare. The other men formed a tight group behind them.

Jennie sidled out on the porch to stand by her husband whereupon Amos's meaty left hand closed over her shoulder. 'You'd better move back inside.'

Jennie crossed her arms over her breasts. She shook her head. 'I'm staying right here.'

Amos's gaze shifted to his left as he let out a breath. 'Have it your way. It's those damn Fisher brothers.'

The Bar F outfit halted less than two feet

from the porch. Leatherwood's gaze reached out to them as he rocked back and forth on high heels. Their leader was a fleshy fellow with a cocky attitude, and Leatherwood felt anger scald his belly when his gaze abruptly settled on a jagged red streak zigzagging down the fellow's right cheek.

The urge to kill straightened him, and Sally's 'Goddamn, what's eating you?' jerked him up short. Reason returned and he forced himself to sink down on the edge of the porch.

Amos's voice grated like pebbles over rock. 'You got a hell of a nerve, Roy. After last night I ought to blow you right out of that saddle.'

Roy Fisher rolled a cigarette. Roy was big but flabby, and his every move was designed to show his importance. He wore a blue shirt, and his chaps were held together by silver conchos. He sat a silvermounted saddle and a Peacemaker's pearl handle jutted from his holster. Roy stuck the quirly to his lips, lit it and, when his blue gaze slanted toward the porch, he flipped the match at Leatherwood's boots.

Leatherwood almost bit the end of his cigar. Rage tightened the big muscles across the top of his shoulders as a spasm rippled down his back. He kept telling himself this wasn't the place. He couldn't take them all even if Sally and Amos backed him, and he had to think of Jennie. Not only that, if he killed Roy, he would have to fight his father. He had to locate Breed and Sam. When he had finished with them, he'd take out the Fisher brothers.

'Heard you had a little trouble last night,' Roy grinned.

Words slipped past Amos's bloodless lips. 'We had trouble all right. You gave it to us.'

'The boys and me never left the ranch.'

'You're a liar.'

'Look, Amos, I didn't ride over here to argue. The old man wants you off Bar F grass.'

'You tell Whit Fisher to go to hell. This is my land.'

'Things could get a lot worse than they were last night.'

'You bastard, what if you'd hit my kids?'

'That's one of the reasons you ought to move on. You got a family to think about.'

'If I could prove you were the one who killed my boy...'

Cigar ash spilled over Leatherwood's lap as the rider on the red mare nudged his mount up to Roy. Carlita had guessed right. These two resembled each other although the one on the mare was younger, lighter and lacked his brother's brashness. This one put a hand on Roy's arm. 'Back off. You know Pa don't want no trouble.'

'To hell with what Pa wants. I can think for myself.'

Bill's angular cheeks quivered. 'Pa will have your hide if anything goes wrong.'

Roy thrashed his quirt against his boot, muttered something under his breath. 'All right, I'll let it pass. But remember what I said, Amos, I want you out of here.'

Sally shot a slug of tobacco juice that

splattered the palomino's right leg. 'Sonny, someone ought to teach you some manners.'

'You think you're the one to do it, Grandma?'

'Sonny, I just might be.'

Roy laughed. His gaze slid over to Leatherwood, steadied there. 'What the hell are you looking at?'

Leatherwood's hand gripped the edge of the porch. He fought the gorge swelling his throat. 'Looks like you ran into a wildcat.'

'Maybe I did. What about it?'

The cigar was falling apart in Leatherwood's mouth. He removed it, spat out some tobacco flakes, and forced a smile. 'Nothing. You're too tough for me.'

Leatherwood watched Roy's shoulders droop as emotion roughened his wilful cheeks. Roy was mulling over that last remark. He'd draw rather than look a fool before his men, but Leatherwood just sat there a frozen smile on his face. Roy glanced right, then left. He felt the pressure and

Leatherwood knew something had to give.

Roy slapped his boot with his quirt again. 'Who are you? What are you doing here?'

'Passing through.'

'Well, keep passing.'

'You can count on it.'

Some of the tension seeped out of Roy's spoiled face. He pulled on his gloves, glared at everyone on the porch.

Leatherwood dropped his mangled cigar butt. His gaze found the scar on Roy's cheek, the silvermounted saddle, the fancy bit, the sharp, fivepointed spurs. One day he would kill him and the one who sat next to him. Still, the younger Fisher had an honest face that lacked his brother's pouty lips and bellicose manner. It was hard to believe the boy had raped Carlita.

Roy flung his quirly into the yard. 'We'll be leaving now. Going to visit the rest of you sheep herders. They'll hear the same thing you heard.'

As they wheeled their horses, Leatherwood rose to his feet. 'Roy, I almost forgot:

I was to deliver a message from Charlie Reardon.'

Roy sawed back on the reins while his startled gaze found Leatherwood. 'What do you know about Charlie Reardon?'

'An acquaintance of mine. Saw him again a few days ago in Benton. He said to tell you he wouldn't be back.'

Roy sucked in his lower lip. One gloved finger traced the scar on his cheek. 'What else did he tell you?'

'Was there anything else to tell?'

Roy kept his gaze on Leatherwood and indecision stencilled his face. 'I don't know about you. Just be sure you keep moving,' he said, and, kicking his mount in the sides, led the Bar F group out of the yard.

Sally hied around to Amos who leaned his shotgun against the wall. 'Those sonsabitches are a couple of sweethearts.'

Amos wiped his face with a bandanna, shoved it in his pocket. 'Bill ain't so bad, but his pa keeps rowelling him. Roy's just like his old man.'

Leatherwood stared at a spot between his boots. 'Amos, make up a supply list while I hitch up the team. Sally and I are going into Llano.'

'They won't sell to you once they see that wagon.'

'Let me worry about that.'

'Whit Fisher won't like it Cliff, I've known Sally a long time and understand her helping, but why are you sticking your neck out?'

'I got my reasons. Make up the list.'

Jennie put a work-worn hand on Amos's shoulder, regarded him from frightened eyes. 'Amos, forget the list. Let's pack up and move on. If we stay here, there'll be more killing. This place ain't worth it. No place is worth it.'

Amos's sunburned face squared determinedly. 'You seem to forget that we got another flock on the way. They're paid for and that took all the money we had.'

'I don't care about the money. Sell the sheep to Miles Walker or give them to him.

You heard what Roy Fisher said. We can't stay here any longer.'

Amos squeezed her hand, removed it from his shoulder. 'I'll get the list,' he said, and lumbered in the house.

Jennie adjusted the comb in her hair. A faraway look crept into her eyes, and her lips trembled. 'Sally, you've known Amos for over twenty years. He never shot a man in his life. Won't you talk to him?'

Sally worked at her chaw, pulled her long nose, shook her head. 'I know him all right, and he's made up his mind. Nothing I can say will change it.'

Jennie stepped up to Leatherwood. 'Cliff, you know about this kind of thing. I can look at you and tell. Can't you convince Amos that Whit Fisher will kill him? I've already lost a son; I don't want to lose my husband.'

Leatherwood studied the toe of his boot. He knew how it felt to lose someone you love. 'I can tell you this: a few days from now Fisher will have more than a few sheep to worry about. Things are going to work out better than you think. Now, you go inside and help Amos.'

Sally pulled at her nose again. Her brown eyes were shrewd, thoughtful and her left hand moved to the handle of her bowie knife. 'You're after the Fishers. When those sonsabitches rode up, I saw something in your face that made me quiver, and there ain't a lot that will make me quiver.'

Leatherwood removed a cigar from his vest pocket, trimmed the end with his Barlow. 'Let's hitch up a team. If we move, we can reach Llano by noon.'

# 7

Leatherwood crossed the walk between the railing and the store with Sally shuffling behind. He plucked a folded length of paper from his vest pocket and extended it toward the store-keeper.

'Here's a list of supplies we need.'

The store-keeper rammed his tobacco pouch into his pocket, held a match to his pipe. 'Don't recall seeing you folks before.'

'Just passing through. This is a cash order.'

'That looks like Amos White's wagon.'

'What of it? You're here to sell; we're here to buy.'

'I don't sell to sheep herders or their friends.'

A smile played across Leatherwood's lips. He looked down from his six foot two inch height, and his smile broadened. 'Do you fill the list or do we fill it?'

The store-keeper eyed Leatherwood's broad shoulders, the gun at his hip. His uneasy gaze flicked to Sally who stood straddle-legged and unsmiling. 'Look, I don't want no trouble, but Mister Fisher told me not to sell to you people.'

Sally spat out a hunk of tobacco juice that landed near the store-keeper's right boot. 'Then it comes down to who you want to please most: us or Mister Fisher.'

Smoke poured from the corn cob as the storekeeper glanced hurriedly up and down the street. 'All right, I'll fill it. But Mister Fisher ain't gonna like it.'

Leatherwood leaned his back against the counter, lit a cigar. He crossed his arms over his chest and pretended to ignore the store-keeper. The smells of coffee, cheese, and molasses reached out to him, and the odour of leather and canvas percolated throughout the store. As Sally ambled over to look at a pile of bull whips, Leatherwood heard the store-keeper moving around in the next room. Through the window he saw a man and woman wheel into the bank and, across the street, two men stepped from the cafe, mounted up and loped out of town.

He lowered his head and smoke drifted up across his face. He wondered if he'd made the right move this morning mentioning Charlie Reardon. The Fisher kid hadn't seemed alarmed, only surprised, but he would carry the tale to the 'breed and Sam. That could make it more difficult to take them off guard, but he supposed it made no difference. He would take them one way or another.

Sally stomped down to him. 'I knew you were after Breed and Sam, but I can't see how the Fishers fit in.'

'Who said they did?'

'I heard what you told Roy this morning. I saw that look on his face. Why don't you let me in on it?'

He shrugged and glanced away. Nature had been unkind to Sally. With her protruding ears, homely face, broad shoulders and big hands, she should have been a man. There wasn't a thing attractive about her. Still, she had something that beat physical charm. She was honest, direct, above board. Those were qualities time wouldn't erode.

As a horseman jogged by, a tingle ran up Leatherwood's back.

The rider was a rangy, muscular-built black. A hat with a Montana peak shaded his face, and he wore a dirty flannel shirt and faded denims. Leatherwood had never seen Sam, but instinctively knew this was the man. He glanced at Sally, noticed that her attention stayed on the store-keeper who had half filled the order. Across the way, the black man pulled in at the saloon, dismounted and waddled through the swinging doors.

Leatherwood kept his voice normal. 'Think I'll step across the street and grab a beer.'

Sally straightened up from the counter. 'Good idea.'

'You'd better stay here. Make sure that order's filled.'

'Right. I'll be over in a few minutes.'

Leatherwood shouldered outside. He saw Sam's mustang tied to the saloon's hitching rail, observed the empty street. He flipped his cigar butt into the dirt and hiked over the road where he rammed through the saloon doors pausing just inside while his eyes adjusted to the light. A bald-headed bartender wiped the mahogany's center. To his right, Sam sipped his beer and, further down the bar, two townsmen chatted over drinks. Except for a bored gambler playing solitaire at the room's far end, the saloon was empty.

About three feet from where Sam drank his beer, Leatherwood eased in at the bar and called for a drink. After putting a bottle and glass before him, the bartender returned to wiping glasses.

The room smelled of old sweat and smoke. Leatherwood sampled the whiskey. He placed his glass on the counter and

94

glared in the black man's direction.

Sam slid a pipe and pouch from his hip pocket, filled the pipe, and lit it. Abruptly, he became aware of Leatherwood's stare and glanced down the bar. The man's full lips broadened in a smile that revealed straight, white teeth. 'Good afternoon. Fine day for a cool one.'

Leatherwood bit off the tip of a cigar and spat it on the floor. His unyielding gaze fixed on the man before him.

Sam pushed his hat back from his forehead, nervously adjusted his collar, trying to figure this out. He'd made a friendly overture and Leatherwood hadn't responded. That had him thinking, sent his mind tunnelling off in different directions in an effort to sort out why he was the object of so much hostility.

From the corner of one eye, Sam studied him. He dipped his gaze back to the front and scratched his neck while his brow crinkled in concentration.

Leatherwood didn't take his attention off

his man. He had positioned himself to Sam's left and in order to draw, Sam would have to make a half-turn, whereas Leatherwood had a straight shot.

Sam glanced his way again. 'I don't think I know you.'

'I know you. You're Sam.'

The black man flashed a friendly, outgoing grin. 'That's right. How'd you know?'

'Charlie Reardon told me.'

'You a friend of Charlie's?'

'You were with Charlie, Breed and the Fishers when they killed an old man and raped a young girl.'

The black man flattened both hands on the counter as strain bunched his cheeks. 'I don't know what you're talking about.'

'Those folks meant a lot to me. You and your friends made a big mistake.'

Sam looked up and down the bar, then glanced back at Leatherwood. There was no fear in his gaze, only bewilderment. 'Who are you?'

'What difference does it make? Now, go for your gun, you yellow dog.'

The black man's hands shot straight up as he called to the bartender, 'This fellow's loco. If he shoots me, it's murder.'

The barkeep heeled in their direction. His mouth dropped open. Down the bar, the two townsmen became aware of the situation and leaped back from the mahogany. The bartender stared at Leatherwood. 'I don't know what's eating you, but I don't want no trouble in here.'

'There ain't gonna be no trouble,' Sam said. He whirled around, hands still high in the air, and armed through the swinging doors.

Leatherwood blasted through those doors, crossed the boardwalk, and caught Sam's shoulder when he tried to spring up on his horse. Leatherwood spun him around, slammed a fist into his mouth. Sam hit the ground. He lay there, blood seeping out of his smashed lips, while Leatherwood glared down at him.

'Now you can stand up and reach for that gun or lie there while I blow your head off. It makes no difference to me.'

'It makes a great deal of difference to me.'

Leatherwood half-turned to see a pot-bellied man wearing a marshal's badge holding a pistol in his right hand. Reason came back then and he cursed himself for a fool. The marshal undoubtedly belonged to the Bar F, and Leatherwood was caught between the law and the black man.

The marshal kept his gun on Leatherwood, his face flat and non-committal. 'Sam, mount that horse and ride out of here.'

The marshal waited until Sam gained his saddle and spurred the mustang upstreet. Then, he reholstered his revolver. 'I don't know who you are or what your problem is, but I don't want any killing in Llano. Now, get on about your business.'

Leatherwood tramped over the street toward the mercantile. The situation had changed abruptly. He had lost the initiative. The next move was up to Whit Fisher.

Fisher occupied one of the four rockers scattered along the porch. His Stetson was cocked so that it shaded his upper face and he sucked at his empty pipe, sighing with satisfaction. This spread was his life. Every sight and smell and sound had its special place in his memory. When he sat here, his thoughts often tumbled back to the days when he and Ruby had started an empire.

Someday all this would belong to Roy and Bill, but the thought brought a frown to his forehead. Roy was too proud; Bill, too soft-hearted. He often wondered if they could hold the ranch together. He'd done his best by them but somehow he'd failed. If only Ruby had lived. He'd needed help, the kind only a woman could give. It hurt to think that what he'd devoted his life to might slip away because of his weak sons. Take the sheep herders squatting on the north end of his range: neither Roy nor Bill had the slightest idea of how to handle that problem.

Hoofbeats funnelled in from the east and Whit glanced up as Joel Watts trotted into the yard. Watts drew up at the porch, heaved his overweight frame from the saddle and climbed the steps.

Whit nodded. 'What brings you way out here?'

The marshal removed his hat, wiped his face with his bandanna. 'I heard something in town I thought might interest you.'

Whit tapped some tobacco into his pipe. 'Let's have it.'

'Around noon some stranger tried to kill that black man you hired. I didn't hear it, but evidently he said something about the 'breed and those Fisher boys. Something about what they'd done uptrail. He meant to blow Sam's head off.'

'What did this fellow look like?'

'Nothing unusual. I wouldn't have paid any attention to him if it hadn't been for Sam.'

Whit smoked his pipe, fingers drumming the arm of his chair. 'I'll talk to Roy about it. See what's going on. I appreciate your bringing this out, Joel.'

'There's one more thing. This fellow and his partner bought a load of supplies for Amos White.'

Whit sat up straight, slammed a fist against the arm of his chair. 'I told Virgil not to sell those sheep herders any supplies.'

'I don't think he had any choice.'

'Then why didn't you stop it?'

'I didn't know about it until they'd left town.'

'You say he's got a partner?'

'Some woman. According to Virgil she's near forty or fifty and tougher than raw-hide.'

Whit paced to the edge of the porch, stared out across the horizon, then paced back to Watts. 'Maybe those sheep herders have brought in some guns. Maybe that thing with Sam was planned.'

'I wouldn't know. Only telling you what I heard.'

'What do you think?'

Watts shrugged. 'I don't think he's a gunslinger. He ain't got the look.'

Fisher regarded a spot midway between the marshal's boots. 'You ride on back to town. Keep your eyes open.'

Whit sank back into his chair, pipe smoke rising in gentle puffs. A sudden chill touched him and he slapped a palm against his knee. It had something to do with those marks on Roy's face.

An hour later found Whit perched on the front stoop whittling at a piece of oak. Whittling was his hobby. He never made anything, just cut notches and shaved off long curls of wood. He heard horses and soon Roy and six Bar F riders trotted into the yard. Roy dismounted at the house, handed his reins to a cowboy and swaggered over to join his father.

Whit closed his knife, stuck it in his pocket, and lay the chunk of oak on the step. 'Where's your brother?'

Roy shrugged, dropped down by his dad. 'Don't know. He said he had some business to 'tend to after we left White's. I haven't seen him since.'

Whit tugged at the heavy gold clasp of his bandanna. 'Well, we won't wait for him. I want to know what you and your brother stumbled into uptrail?'

'I told you, Pa. Nothing.'

'I'm tired of your lies. A stranger tried to kill Sam today. He's after the 'breed, you and Bill.'

Roy looked down at his hands for a long moment, then peeled off his gloves. 'What does this stranger look like?'

'I don't know anything about him.'

'There was a stranger – two of them – at White's today.'

'Two of them?'

Roy chuckled. 'Nothing to worry about. I braced the man. The other one was some loud-mouthed old woman.'

'You're stupid, boy. Stupid. Quit beating around the bush and tell me what happened.'

Roy stared out into the yard. He rubbed his hands up and down his thighs as his

Adam's apple jumped in his throat. 'Pa, it ain't like it sounds. It was an accident. We'd been drinking.'

Whit grabbed his son's upper arm. 'What happened?'

'We rode by this little ranch about sundown and stopped to water our horses. There was an old man there, a Mexican, and he asked us to stay for supper. He had a real pretty daughter. Like I said, Pa, we'd been drinking.'

Whit closed his eyes; his lips disappeared under pressure. He felt cold sitting there in the late evening sun.

'Pa, they were just a couple of Mexicans.'

'Just a couple of Mexicans. Well, boy, they were more than that to somebody. Don't I have enough trouble with these sheep herders?'

'I told you, Pa. You don't have to worry. I already braced him.'

'Yeah. With six of my men backing you. You fool. If he'd take on Sam, he ain't afraid of you.'

'I can take care of myself.'

'If you were only half as tough as you think you are. Well, I'll give him Breed, Sam and Charlie and pay him off for you two.'

'Charlie's gone, Pa. He ain't coming back.'

'That's the first I heard of it.'

'The stranger told me. Said Charlie sent word he wouldn't be back.'

Whit grunted, fingered his gold clasp. 'You can bet on it. He's dead. Get out of my sight. I've got to think about this.'

As Roy reached his feet, Whit dug his pipe from his pocket, filled it with tobacco. He heard Roy's boots thump over the porch, heard the door open, close. He'd known something was wrong the moment they'd returned, but he'd never have guessed this. He was a decent, reasonable man. He'd tried to raise decent, reasonable sons, but he'd failed. He had to talk to that stranger. Reach some kind of accord. Roy and Bill were wrong, but they still were his sons. He couldn't stand by and let someone kill them. The other fellow was in the right and had to be satisfied if possible. He wasn't like those sheep herders who had no rights, who had come into this country and tried to take something that belonged to him.

He was smoking his third pipe when Bill cantered into the yard. He found it hard to believe Bill had been part of this. Frankly, Bill was too weak, too soft, too easily swayed by his brother. Bill dismounted at the porch, sat down by his father.

'Something bothering you, Pa?'

'You and your brother .... I found out about the trouble you two and those saddle bums caused.'

Bill's gaze rolled away from his father. He studied the steps, toyed with the small rowel on his Texas spur. 'It was an accident, Pa.'

'So I've heard. You remember that stranger over at White's?'

'Yes, sir.'

'He's a friend of those people.'

'I knew there was something odd about him. He kept staring at Roy.'

'Now you know why.'

'I didn't touch that girl, Pa, I swear I didn't.'

'You didn't stop anybody from touching her.'

'I don't know how it happened. I don't know what Roy was thinking about.'

'It's too late to cry now. Go inside and wash up. It's about supper-time.'

# 8

Cigar jutting from his teeth, Cliff Leatherwood sat on the top stoop of White's porch.
He pulled out his horologe, noted it was 9
a.m. and, giving the voluptuous nude an
appreciative examination, snapped the cover
and returned the watch to his pocket. The
sun warmed him from the waist down, so he
moved back into one of the rockers to
escape the heat. Footsteps shuffled and he
glanced over his shoulder as Sally and Amos
walked from the house.

Sally ran short, gnarled fingers over her
dirty grey hair. Jennie had gathered it into a
ponytail, and Sally's flaring ears protruded
more than ever. 'What do we do now, Cliff?'

'I'm moving on.'

Sally shoved her thumbs under her wide
leather belt. 'I figure to move with you.'

Amos worked at his chewing tobacco. His lips curved down and he looked harassed and unhappy. 'I wish you two would stick around. We got a bunch of sheep arriving in a couple of days. God knows what Whit Fisher will do.'

Leatherwood removed the cigar from his teeth. 'I know you got problems, Amos, but I got to tend my own fences.'

'I suppose everybody has. Just wishing.'

Sally bit off a chew of Twist. 'Cliff's after the Fisher boys. He might be more help than you think.'

Amos squared around to face Leatherwood. 'What's she talking about?'

'Just talk.'

'I've known her too long for that. What are you hinting at, Sally?'

'Goddamn if I know, Cliff don't confide in me. But I saw the surprise on that Fisher boy's face yesterday, and when Cliff mentioned Reardon, I saw something in Cliff's eye.'

'Cliff,' Amos said, 'if you're after the

Fishers, you might do better to throw in with us.'

'I thought about it, but you've got enough trouble.'

Amos scuffed at his jaw. 'I know a lot about Whit Fisher. Maybe we could help each other.'

Leatherwood studied his cigar. Then he proceeded to tell what happened at Manuel's, what happened to Charlie, plus what happened in town with Sam.

Amos shifted his chaw from his right to his left jaw. He glanced at Sally who'd leaned back against the wall and crossed her arms over her breasts. 'What's your interest?'

'That Charlie Reardon was worth two hundred and fifty bucks. I figure Cliff owes me something.'

'When did you take up bounty hunting?'

'When I missed out on a load of freight. I'm dead broke.'

'I'm sorry you missed Charlie, but it's good seeing you again. I know Cliff's got to ride, but why don't you stay?'

'Hell, I ain't no sheep herder.'

'You could be.' Amos turned away. He fingered the stubble covering his cheeks, stared down into the yard. 'You know, if anything happens to this flock, I'm finished.'

'It would be the best thing that ever happened to us.'

They glanced around to see Jennie standing in the doorway. Her gingham dress fell shapelessly around her bulky form. Her round countenance looked tired and sleepy. 'We'd be smart to leave, too.'

'Now, woman, why would you say that?'

'Because it's the truth. Whit Fisher means to have this land regardless. If we stay here, somebody else is going to die.'

Amos hooked his thumbs in his suspenders. 'He ain't running me off my place.'

'This place is nothing but a four-room shack. There's nothing here worth dying for.'

Amos's teeth clicked. His eyes smouldered. 'Somebody's already died. I aim to make Whit Fisher pay for it.'

'Nothing will bring Tom back. This is all my fault. If it wasn't for me, we wouldn't be here.'

'Now hush that kind of talk. It ain't your fault. It's Whit Fisher's.'

Jennie's hand rose to her lips. Her eyes continued to stare off into space. 'I'm the one who kept harping on a place of our own.'

'Sally, what can you do with a woman like this? You can't talk sense to her.'

Leatherwood crossed his legs, flicked the ash from his cigar. He liked these people. He wished he could help them. But he couldn't get trapped in this affair. His debt was to Manuel and Carlita.

Sally's voice sliced through his reflections. 'There's a rider coming.'

Leatherwood spotted a single horseman silhouetted against the smoky horizon. 'You got good eyes.'

Amos pumped into the house, returned

with a shotgun cradled in his right arm. 'He's coming from the wrong direction.'

Jennie adjusted the comb in her hair. Her workworn hands closed at her sides. 'The Fishers always ride in a gang. Never alone.'

The cowboy reined up at the porch. He looked at Leatherwood. 'Mister Fisher wants to talk to you. He's at the Bar F.'

Leatherwood nodded. 'Tell him I'll be there.'

'He was wondering about your name.'

'Leatherwood. Cliff Leatherwood.'

The cowboy raised two fingers in a salute, wheeled and cantered out of the yard. The four of them sat there in curious silence until he rode out of earshot.

'I wonder what that coyote is up to?' Sally said.

Amos said, 'Whatever it is, it ain't good. You're not going are you, Cliff?'

'Why not? The man's waiting.'

Sally stared at him like he had two heads. 'Are you crazy? Hell, it's a setup. You think that sonofabitch is gonna say "Hello" and let you ride out of there?'

Jennie put a hand on Leatherwood's arm. Her lips trembled. 'She's right, Cliff. You can't trust Whit Fisher.'

'I don't aim to, but if he wanted trouble why didn't he send his whole crew after me?'

'Because he'd have a fight on his hands,' Amos muttered.

'There's twenty of them, four of us. It wouldn't be much of a fight.'

Sally hitched up her trousers. 'I'll go with you.'

'You weren't invited. Besides, Amos and Jennie might need you.'

'Bullshit! You ain't leaving without me. You might decide not to come back. Then I'm out of my share of that reward money.'

Leatherwood shook his head in exasperation. 'I'll be back tonight. Now, I'm going to saddle Trooper and ride over there.' Stepping off the porch, he hiked to the barn without bothering to look back. Sally meant well, but he didn't need her. Like he'd said, if Fisher had wanted trouble, he'd come looking for it.

Minutes later, after turning to wave at the three people crowding the porch, Leatherwood trotted out of the yard. It had been a long time since anyone had worried about Cliff Leatherwood, and that gave him another reason to finish this. Losing his sons and gunmen, Whit Fisher just might begin to question how important this land was.

He reined toward the mountains. The grass, lush and thick, carpeted Trooper's hoofbeats. Far off, a line of cottonwoods marked the river. Overhead, the sky stretched out like a roll of seamless carpet and the sun carved a yellow hole in the sky. He passed a salt lick, a waterhole, and noted how cattle hoofs had chopped up the sod around the little pond. Eastward, to his left, cattle dotted the land, and cow birds formed black specks against the sky.

At late afternoon, he reached the Bar F. Trooper jogged by the barn, walked across the yard and turned the corner of the big house. On the front porch, a man in a brown Stetson and flannel shirt sat in one of the rockers. The man's lazy gaze watched Leatherwood as he dismounted. Leatherwood tipped back his hat and had his first look at Whit Fisher. He saw a man with grey eyes steadily observing him from a stern, impassive face. The nose on that face had been broken; two, long lines ran from the nostrils to the lips.

'Have a seat. I'd about given up on you.'

Leatherwood took out a cigar, bit into it, and considered the men fanning out from among the trees. A faint alarm cooled the back of his neck. He removed a block of matches from his vest pocket, broke off a match, and fired his cigar.

He listened intently for sounds from inside the house, but heard nothing. He didn't like the feel of it. Amos and Sally had guessed right: riding out might be a lot more difficult than riding in.

Whit shaped a point on a chunk of oak. 'I guess you know why you're here?'

'Why don't you tell me.'

Whit slumped lower in his chair, thoughtfully sharpening the stick. Outwardly he seemed completely at ease, but the pulse in his neck beat slow and heavy while a certain rigidity stiffened his shoulders.

'There's no excuse for what those boys of mine did. I want to make it up to you.'

Leatherwood raised his left arm so that his elbow sat on the arm of the chair. The derringer was a weight on his wrist, a comfortable, reassuring weight. Again, Leatherwood considered the men half hidden in the oaks. Whit wasn't taking any chances of things not going his way.

Whit's grey eyes probed him, and Leatherwood was surprised at the compassion in the rancher's face. 'I know what it costs to lose somebody, but nothing changes that loss. Nothing's gonna bring that old man and his daughter ...'

'Granddaughter.'

'...granddaughter back. I know how you

feel. You want to kill somebody and I don't blame you. In your place I would too. But try to see this my way: those two boys are all I've got.'

'And you want me to forget what happened.'

'I'll give you the 'breed and Sam. They caused most of the trouble anyway.'

'From those marks on Roy's face, I'm not sure we agree.'

Emotion shortened Whit's lips. He tossed the stick aside, closed his knife and thrust it in his pocket. 'Look, I'm trying to reason with you. I know how you feel and I don't want to kill you, but if I have to, I will.'

Leatherwood blew out a long streamer of smoke. Rising, he walked to the end of the porch. A man centered the bunkhouse doorway. The fellow's hat sat low over his forehead, but Leatherwood could feel the intensity of the gaze beating from under that brim. He drew slowly on his cigar wondering how many hands occupied the bunkhouse.

Whit clumped down to stand beside him. 'I intend to run those sheep herders off. You can have that land. I'll even stock it with cattle. Maybe that will make up for what my boys did.'

Leatherwood's molars tore into the cigar. Before him, he saw Manuel's bloodless face, Carlita's misshapen one. He glanced down at Whit knowing he dealt with a man who'd always had his way. Whit wanted to do what he thought was right; but in case of refusal, he had all the other options covered.

Leatherwood shook his head. 'I'm afraid it won't wash.'

'Don't be a fool. You don't think I'm going to let you ride out of here unless this is settled? How much is your life worth?'

'How much is yours worth?'

The first trace of doubt blunted the contours of Whit's face. He seemed puzzled. 'You couldn't pull that pistol fast enough. You're covered.'

Leatherwood crossed his arms over his chest, right arm under his left in such a way that Whit Fisher could see the derringer clipped to his wrist. 'I can pull that fast enough.'

Uncertainty deepened the lines driving down Whit's cheeks as he fumbled with his gold clasp. 'I wanted to reason with you, but you're a fool just like those sheep herders. Now you'll have to take the consequences.'

Leatherwood spoke in a voice that was meant to carry. 'Let's walk down to the barn and find you a horse.'

Whit glanced at the oaks; he eyed the man standing in the bunkhouse doorway. His lips closed on the pipe stem and refusal tightened his lips, but something in Leatherwood's demeanour changed his mind.

Leatherwood dropped a step behind the rancher. When they passed the hitching post, he gathered up Trooper's reins and moved so that the big gelding shielded him from the trees. As he and Whit turned the corner, he positioned the grey so that the horse still covered him. The barn, a big shed-like affair, loomed twenty-five yards ahead of them. The hayloft doors swung wide on to the yard. Leatherwood studied them, but the shade was too deep. He couldn't tell if anyone was hiding up there.

They reached the barn, halted just outside the open doors with the two men from the bunkhouse poised off to their left. Leatherwood dropped Trooper's reins, crossed his arms in a casual gesture. He couldn't ease the dryness in his mouth and he spat the mangled cigar butt to the ground. Whit said, 'You'll never make it', whereupon Leatherwood gave him a relentless stare. 'If I don't, neither will you.'

Leatherwood's head tilted toward the barn. 'We're going to walk in there and find you a horse. Remember, how this ends is up to you.'

They entered the barn's shaded runway. Coming in out of the bright sunlight made the barn seem darker than it really was; Leatherwood had difficulty seeing. As they approached a line of stalls, he shoved Whit toward the first one. Whit stumbled into it, manoeuvered a bit into a horse's mouth, and lifted the reins over its ears. As Whit reached for a saddle blanket, Leatherwood's gaze swept both sides of the hayloft. The coolness solidified at the base of his neck. He heeled around so that he could see through the open doorway, noted that a group of men formed a semi-circle near the rear of the house. He heard a saddle land on a horse's back, heard leather squeak as Whit tightened the cinch. Then Whit led his horse into the runway.

Leatherwood reconsidered the hayloft. His lips felt dry; his ears ached from strain. 'Stay just ahead of me. When we reach my horse, we both mount up.'

Leatherwood searched the loft again, keened all his senses to catch some sound or movement up there. They reached the doorway and walked into the sunlit yard. A man coughed near the house. One of the hands by the corral yelled, 'Mister Fisher, is everything all right?'

Whit waved in that direction. 'Every-

122

thing's fine,' he said and abruptly wheeled toward Leatherwood and rammed a shoulder into Cliff's ribcage. Leatherwood stumbled backwards. He grabbed a fistful of Whit's shirt and reached for his revolver. As the gun cleared leather, hot pain seared Leatherwood's scalp and he heard a muffled explosion. Then his knees seemed to fall out from under him as he pitched into black-ness.

# 9

Leatherwood groaned. Someone kept tapping the top of his head and pain encompassed him. He lay in a black hole and that hole seemed to close in on him. He tried to open his eyes, tried to see some light at the top of the chasm, but he was blind, helpless against the waves of pain that swept over him. He groped around until his fingers dug into the sides of the pit, and he began the slow, agonizing climb to the top. The darkness swirled around him, broken by splinters of light. Those splinters pierced his eyelids, probed like needles at his brain.

His eyelids flickered half-open, and he saw that the splinters of light came from a lamp burning on a bottomed-up barrel. The shape of the lamp wavered and he could not be sure if he saw one lamp or three. He closed his eyes, fought the sickness in his throat and chest. He opened his eyes again, saw an unpainted ceiling. He heard voices then. He brought a hand up across his face, felt something sticky, and followed that stickiness up into his hair. As he rolled his head right, the tapping increased in intensity. Then the lamp didn't waver any more and his gaze focused on Whit Fisher and the two cowboys sitting beyond him.

Whit pushed to his feet and walked over to the bunk. 'I told you you'd never make it.'

Leatherwood attempted to raise up on his elbows, but the lamp wavered again. It was hard to breathe.

Whit removed the pipe from his mouth, his features bland and noncommittal. 'You were lucky. A quarter of an inch lower and the top of your head would be gone. This could have been so simple if you'd accepted my offer.'

'Maybe I'll accept it now.'

Whit laughed. 'Still got your sense of humor.'

Leatherwood made it up on his elbows. His head still throbbed, but some of his strength had returned. He glanced beyond Whit to the two cowboys who sat near the lamp. One of them was the heavy-set fellow who had watched him earlier from the bunkhouse The other one he didn't recognize.

Whit shook his head, pushed his pipe into his vest pocket. 'You're a problem. I don't know exactly what to do.'

'Let's not kid each other. After killing an unarmed boy guarding a bunch of sheep, you know what you're going to do.'

Whit's mouth smashed into a long line. 'I had nothing to do with killing that boy. I wanted to reason with those people. If somebody got hurt, it's not my fault. Now, you get some rest. You'll need it.' Whit heeled around to the table. 'Ed, you and Cleve keep your eyes on him. I'm going over to the house and get some sleep.'

Leatherwood lay on the cot, his head pounding. The inside of his mouth felt ridged and it was hard to swallow. He closed his eyes against the light. Fisher was right. The best thing he could do was rest. He was too weak to even think of escape. But the pounding in his head wouldn't stop and he couldn't switch off his brain. A chair screeched against the flooring and he shot a quick look at the guards. The man called Cleve had stood up and crossed to the doorway. He closed his eyes again, heard a match scratch across wood, caught the pungent odor of tobacco. He wondered how Fisher would handle this. Whit could have killed him out there in the yard. Instead, the rancher had hauled him in here. Maybe Whit couldn't shoot a man cold, but he had no doubt about Whit's boys. Not after what they'd done to Manuel and Carlita.

Movement brought Leatherwood awake; his eyes opened to morning. He glanced at the guards, saw they had been replaced by a tall fellow with a moustache. Leatherwood sat up on the side of the bed, waited for sleep to clear from his brain. He was dizzy, but the pain was gone. Wondering what time it was, he pulled out his horologe. Seven o'clock. He'd been out for four hours. He replaced the watch, noticed that his derringer was missing.

The moustached fellow removed a cigarette from his mouth. 'You want something to eat?'

'I guess so.'

'You can wash up outside.'

Leatherwood got to his feet, shuffled past his captor who followed him into the yard. The sky was overcast; the smell of rain flavored the breeze. His guard directed him to the rear of the big house where he found a bucket and washpan. He poured water into the pan, washed the blood from his cheek. The cowboy motioned him inside where they walked through the kitchen into a dining area. The room was empty. He sat on one side of a table while the moustached cowboy sat on the other. Moments later, a Chinaman brought eggs, steak and coffee.

After breakfast, they recrossed the yard to

the tackroom. Leatherwood sat on the edge of a bunk and lit a cigar. The other man positioned his chair near the doorway where he rolled a cigarette. Leatherwood lay back and puffed on his cigar. The food had made a new man of him, but he could do nothing but lie here and wait for an opportunity that might not come.

About an hour later, Whit Fisher entered the room. He motioned his man outside and dropped into the empty chair. 'How do you feel?'

'Pretty weak,' Leatherwood lied.

'You might as well know. The only thing I can do is hand you over to Breed and Sam.'

'I guess I pegged you wrong. I thought you had enough guts to do your own dirty work.'

'I didn't get where I am by being faint-hearted, but I don't need any unnecessary problems.'

Leatherwood grunted. He stared at the ceiling and digested this. If he had the opportunity, it would come when they moved him. Once he got astride Trooper, the situation would change. The horse was damn near human. It depended on how many men accompanied him. If it was only two, he had a chance.

A group of horsemen trotted out of the yard. Leatherwood smoked a cigar. Boredom set in, and he wondered how long Fisher meant to keep him here. Then he slept awhile.

Later, voices sounded from outside and Roy and Bill Fisher stepped into the tackroom. They stopped just inside the door where Roy's pouty lips formed a huge smile. 'Well, look who's here. I told you he wasn't so tough, Pa.'

Whit glanced up from his whittling. His features contracted in a sour grimace. 'You're a fool, boy.'

Anger spotted Roy's cheeks, and he made a show of stripping off his buckskin gloves. Bill glanced from Leatherwood to his father. His forehead puckered thoughtfully as he took out papers and a sack of Bull Durham.

'I guess you two have been playing cards

nearly all night.'

Roy rested his hand on his pearl-handled Peacemaker. He gave his father an amused glance. 'There's a new bunch of sheep coming in.'

Whit stopped his whittling. 'You sure?'

'They'll be nearing Thunder Gap this afternoon.'

Whit tossed his stick to the floor. He folded his knife, put it in his pocket. 'They just won't learn, will they.'

Roy slapped his quirt against his leg. 'Why don't you let me take a few men and run them off? Finish this thing?'

'It may come to that. God knows I've tried to avoid it.'

'Goddamn it, Pa. They ain't gonna run. We ain't gonna do nothing and they know it.'

'That's enough. You know I don't allow cussing on this place.'

Roy looked at Leatherwood. 'What about him?'

'I'll turn him over to the 'breed and Sam.'

131

Bill drew on his cigarette. A strained exhaustion etched his cheeks and he looked at the floor. He stood there for a moment as though he didn't want anyone to see the thoughts working behind his face. When he glanced up, he threw Leatherwood a long glance before wheeling into the yard.

Whit stuck his pipe in his mouth, talked around it. 'Roy, I want you to take some men over to Box Canyon. Turn them over to Breed and tell him to stop those sheep.'

'It's no good, Pa. They'll just send for more.'

Whit jerked erect. His hands hung stiffly at his sides. 'This is their last chance. If they don't move on, we'll do it your way.'

Roy tapped his quirt against his leg. Grinned at Leatherwood. 'Does he go with me?'

'Not now. I want those sheep handled first.'

Sally stood on the edge of the porch gazing at the ten o'clock sun. She sucked at the plug of tobacco in her cheek, turned and paced back in the house where she walked into the kitchen and sank down at the table.

Amos stirred a spoonful of sugar into his coffee, laid the spoon on the table. 'Do you think he's dead?'

Sally let out a long breath, removed the plug from her mouth and threw it in the trash barrel. 'I don't know. Why wouldn't he let me go with him?'

Amos ran a hand through his receding hairline. 'Then we'd have two of you to worry about.'

Jennie stirred at her coffee absent-mindedly. The flesh around her jawline sagged and her eyes looked old. 'How many more are going to die before we leave this country?'

From the tack-room, Cliff Leatherwood heard voices murmuring in the yard; he caught the clatter of hoofs, then silence descended over the Bar F. He lay on his right side in the bunk and watched moonfaced Ed straddle a chair in the doorway.

Ed reached his feet. His wide frame shut off the sunlight and one hand lingered over a birthmark that purpled his left cheek. 'Let's get some grub. It's been a long morning.'

Leatherwood rolled off the bunk. He pretended to sway a little as he reached his feet. Ed noticed that sway and some of the caution left his bored countenance. Leatherwood shuffled over the room as if drawing on his last reserve of strength while Ed backed into the yard giving him space to clear the room. Blinking his eyes against the sunlight, Leatherwood paused just outside the doorway. Except for the two of them, the yard was empty and the only sound was the screech of an oak limb against the side of the house. Ed motioned that way. Leatherwood plodded over the yard. The bunkhouse reared off to his right, but the door was closed and he had a feeling it was empty, that the ranch was deserted except for the two of them.

He mounted the steps, traversed the kitchen, and sat at the long dining-table. Seconds later, the Chinaman brought in two plates heaped with beef and beans. He sat the plates before them, faded into the kitchen and returned with coffee and biscuits. Leatherwood toyed with his food. He sensed that only Ed stood between him and freedom. The Chinaman didn't worry him. The man was too old, too slow to be a factor. Ed was another matter. The beefy, muscular cowboy looked tough; Whit Fisher must have thought he could handle things or he wouldn't have left him alone. Leatherwood glanced through lowered lids at the man across the table. He didn't look like someone who would be caught off guard easily.

Leatherwood cleaned his plate, poured a second cup of coffee. He lit a cigar as Ed shoved back from the table. He brought the cup to his lips, swallowed. The coffee was hot and he considered hurling it in Ed's face. Their gaze met over the edge of the cup. Leatherwood saw a flicker in Ed's eyes that told him the cowboy knew what he was thinking. A smile tugged at Ed's lips. He stood up. 'Let's get back to the tack-room.'

Leatherwood led the way back to the tack-room where Leatherwood sat on the narrow cot. Ed regained his chair, rolled a cigarette, held a match to it. 'You got any ideas, forget them. You ain't going nowhere until Mr Fisher gets back.'

The cigar sat solidly between Leatherwood's teeth. He noticed his saddle-bags in the corner, his six-gun and belt beside them. He drew on the cigar, mind working. A good seven feet separated him from the Bar F cowboy. He'd get his head blown off if he tried anything. His teeth chomped on the cigar as he tried to think of something to do. The bunch that had ridden out would return tonight. If he got out of this, it would have to be before those men returned. Frankly, his chances didn't look too good.

He lay back on the cot, stared at the

ceiling. In his mind, he formed a picture of the Bar F – the big house, the oak trees, the bunkhouse, the barn next to the room in which he lay. Nothing in that picture suggested any way out of it. He crossed his arms over his chest missing the familiar weight of the derringer usually strapped to his left wrist. After he had finished his cigar, he closed his eyes and pretended to sleep. He heard a match flare as Ed lit a cigarette, caught the man's short grunt of boredom. By now, he was certain he and Ed were the only men on the ranch except for the cook. Tension began to knot in his belly and the big muscles running along the top of his shoulders as the pressure of waiting made it impossible to carry on his pretence of sleep.

He opened his eyes, blinked, stretched his neck as if he were just awakening. His hand rubbed the stubble covering his chin as he sat up and swung his legs to the floor. 'OK if I shave?'

Ed's gaze touched him. A cigar dangled from the corner of his mouth. 'You planning on some visitors?'

'Just something to do. I'm tired of lying here.'

Ed dropped the cigarette to the floor, smudged it out. 'All right. A change will do us both good.'

Leatherwood eased to his feet and, with Ed's careful gaze following every step, he shouldered through the doorway and ambled over the yard to the wash bench where Ed held a position about eight feet to his right.

Ed tossed Leatherwood a razor, hooked his thumbs in his belt as Leatherwood pumped water into the wash pan. He lathered his face and neck and shaved a line from his cheekbone to his jaw. He shaved the other cheek, rinsed the razor, then worked around his chin and mouth, making careful swipes around his throat and Adam's apple. He washed and dried his face, cleaned the razor, turned and tossed it back to Ed. As the cowboy's right hand reached to catch it, Leatherwood grabbed the pan of water, hurled it in Ed's direction and flung his body forward. His hands grabbed for Ed's shirt, but the muscular cowboy just laughed, spun out of Leatherwood's path and as Leatherwood flashed by, brought both hands down at the base of Leatherwood's neck. Shockwaves rocked in Leatherwood's head, the ground rushed up and, smashed him in the face. The smell of dirt flooded his nostrils; the taste of it filled his mouth. When he finally shoved up on his knees, arrow points stabbed the top of his head as Ed circled around in front of him.

A grin split the cowboy's beefy countenance. He tossed Leatherwood a towel, shook his head. 'I figured you had to try me, so I thought I'd give you the chance. Now, wipe the dirt off and let's get back.'

Leatherwood sat on the edge of the cot. Pain hammered his head and he felt sick at the stomach. Ed had out-thought him all along. No wonder he grinned.

A steady drumming brought him struggling

to. He recognized the drumming as hoofbeats and realized he'd been asleep. Darkness gathered in the corners of the room and the light beyond the threshhold had turned dusty grey. Ed still occupied his chair, but fatigue and boredom dulled his meaty face. Leatherwood rolled to a sitting position, pulled out his watch. It was 5.45. The hoofbeats passed the tackroom. Leatherwood breathed easier when he realized it was only one rider.

Boots scuffed over the yard and a young, blackhaired puncher appeared in the doorway. His gaze settled on Leatherwood. 'Who's that?'

'One of the sheep herders.'

'He don't look like no sheep herder to me.'

'He works for them. Rip, take him over and get him something to eat. I got to see a man about a dog. You don't have to worry: I've already knocked the vinegar out of him.'

They walked through the lamplighted kitchen where the Chinaman stirred at what smelled like a pot of stew. Leatherwood took a chair to the right while Rip hunkered down on the left. They were hardly seated before the Chinaman placed stew and coffee before them.

Leatherwood glanced across the table. Rip couldn't be over eighteen. He eyed Leatherwood warily. Leatherwood looked down at his plate, picked up his fork. He had five, maybe six minutes before Ed joined them. He dropped his fork and, when it clattered against the floor, bent down as if to retrieve it. Abruptly be reared upright, his hand flattening against the bottom of the table as he hurled it into Rip's startled face. Leatherwood put his weight behind the table, driving it forward and ramming Rip into the wall. Dishes clattered against the floor, and hot coffee splashed on Leatherwood's left leg. He heard Rip's body *whump* against wood, heard the youngster's strangled oaths. He flung the table aside as Rip slid downward. Blood seeped from the corner of Rip's mouth and stew dribbled down his torn shirt. Leatherwood bent over, jerked the revolver from his holster. The boy was out cold, all the vitality beaten from him by the battering ram that Leatherwood's 220 pounds had propelled into him.

Two giant steps carried Leatherwood into the kitchen where he saw the Chinaman huddled in the far corner, meat cleaver raised in his trembling right hand. As a frightened grimace bared his crooked teeth, the Chinaman's terrified gaze met Cliff Leatherwood's. After one quick glance, Leatherwood hustled through the kitchen doorway. Deep shadows spread over the yard. The bunkhouse was dim on the horizon and the huge oaks formed solid silhouettes against the night. Lamplight poured from the open doorway, outlining Leatherwood's frame as he crossed the back porch. A voice yelled, 'Rip? What's going on in there?' Leatherwood saw Ed's beefy shape lumber toward the house.

Leatherwood leaped into the gloom closing around the back stoop. Ed yelled

142

again. A revolver blasted and yellow flame blazed over the dark. Leatherwood dropped to one knee behind the stoop's protective outline where he waited until Ed burst into the square of yellow extending from the kitchen into the yard. Leatherwood said, 'Drop it.' When Ed thumbed a quick shot that buried itself in the house, Leatherwood squeezed off a round that smashed Ed's throat and bowled him backward.

The acrid smell of smoke and cordite stung Leatherwood's nostrils as he reached his feet and raced over the yard. In the tack-room, he slung Rip's six-gun toward the cot, grabbed his own belt and holster and buckled it around his waist. His left hand closed over his saddle-bags and he dodged outside and into the barn. It was pitch black. He heard horses moving around in their stalls and the dry odor of hay filtered from the loft. Leatherwood struck a match, located a lantern, and fired the wick. Jerking his saddle gear from the wall, he checked the stalls until he found Trooper. Quick hands slipped on the bridle, adjusted the blanket, cinched the saddle. Then Leatherwood was astride the big gelding that pounded down the runway and into the night.

# 10

A nine o'clock sun filtered through the east window, the rays not quite reaching the three people huddled around the small table. Jennie White came in from the kitchen with the coffee pot. She poured three cups, sank down in the empty chair and poured herself a cup. Outside, the laughter of John and Karen rang above the gloom surrounding the table. Miles Walker lighted his pipe, heavy puffs of smoke layering the air. Sally leaned forward on both elbows while Amos added milk to his coffee.

Jennie adjusted her comb. 'Sure you don't want some pie with your coffee, Miles?'

'Had a big breakfast before I left home.'

Amos formed a tent with his short, stubby fingers. His broad, stubborn face, running down into his huge neck and bull-like shoulders, was pale for once, his blue eyes screwed deep in their sockets. 'Goddamn that Whit Fisher. If I could get my hands on his neck, I'd wring it like a chicken's.'

Sally peered from beneath the turned-down rim of her wool hat. 'No reason to act so surprised. Cliff told us what happened last night.'

Amos bared his teeth. 'I know, but I kept hoping he was wrong.'

Miles slurped his coffee. Loss of sleep clouded his grey eyes, and small, tired lines wiggled down his cheeks. 'Not much we can do about the sheep, but what about Rick Pettis? If he leaves, Fisher's going to put more pressure on us although I don't see how we can hang on anyway. We're broke.'

Jennie stirred uninterestedly at her coffee. Her dress was too small for her overweight frame, and her petticoat gleamed through a tear in the seam under her arm. 'I think Rick's the only one in the whole bunch with any sense. There's nothing here for us. Not now.'

146

Amos slammed a fist down on the table so hard that the coffee cups jumped. 'Whit Fisher will never run me off my place. There has to be an answer and we have to find it.'

Karen's squeal reverberated through the window followed by John's high-pitched laugh. Sally finished her coffee, slipped a length of Twist from her pocket and bit off a hunk. She felt worn out and irritable. Cliff had ridden in around eleven last night and they'd chewed the fat until near one. He'd told them about his close call at the Bar F and informed Amos as to Fisher's knowledge of the incoming flock. Then he'd headed that big grey for Llano. He'd shot one of Fisher's hands and the sonofabitch would be looking for him. If he found him here, it might be the excuse Fisher needed to burn Amos out. Cliff had said he'd be safe in Llano because Fisher liked to pretend he operated inside the law. Even though he owned the town, any killing would be seen by a lot of witnesses and that was the kind of publicity Fisher wanted to avoid. Personally, Sally couldn't understand it. The nearest federal law was over 100 miles away and Fisher controlled enough people to back up any story he invented.

She jawed the tobacco around, swallowed the juice. Whit Fisher and his Bar F complicated everything. Otherwise, she and Cliff would have corralled Breed and Sam already. She could have collected her reward money and been on the way home. She didn't mind hauling in Breed and Sam dead. They were a couple of skunks whom somebody should have drilled long ago.

Miles's pipe had gone out and he struck another match. He held the match too long, blew at the flame that singed his fingers. 'I can't figure which way to turn. I don't want to start over again, but Fisher has us backed into a corner.'

Amos ran his fingers along the receding line of his stiff, grey hair. The pressure of these last weeks had thinned his bluff countenance, left a harassed glint in his eyes. 'We're down, but we ain't out. We still

148

own the land.'

Sally sucked at her chew as her masculine face puckered thoughtfully. 'Would seven hundred and fifty dollars bring you out?'

Amos's gaze slanted in her direction. He scuffed at his nose. 'You got that kind of money?'

'Maybe I can get it.'

Amos scuffed at his nose again, looked at Miles. Miles puffed thoughtfully on his pipe, his lanky features marked with interest. Amos swung back to Sally. His fingers formed another peak, and he nodded almost imperceptibly. 'Seven hundred and fifty would put us back in business, but we can't guarantee you'd get your money back.'

'Goddamn it, I ain't worried about the money.'

Amos cleared his throat. He stared down at his coffee. 'I thought you said you was broke?'

'I also said there was reward money on Breed and Sam.'

'After what Cliff told me, I don't think he's gonna let us take them. Besides, I'm not too sure we could. We're not gunfighters, and they got the Bar F behind them.'

Miles laid his briar on the table. 'Amos is right. We move on those two and that'll give Whit Fisher an excuse to come down on us.'

'Bullshit. Cliff and I will take care of Breed and Sam.'

Amos stuck his thumbs in his red suspenders, rocked upright in his chair. 'How you know Cliff will go along with it? You and me been friends for years, Sally; Cliff, he don't owe me nothing.'

'All he wants is those two sonsabitches dead. He don't care about the money.'

Amos stared at his coffee again while Miles scraped out his pipe and packed in a fresh load of tobacco. Jennie's lantern jaw trembled. She touched her hair, a sad, troubled expression moistening her eyes. 'Amos, if you think anything of me and those children out there, you'll forget that money. We've lost Tom: that's enough.'

'But Jennie...'

'Daddy! Daddy! There's a bunch of men riding this way,' John yelled.

Amos's chair screeched across the floor. Miles leaped to his feet and Jennie stood upright, alarm smearing her face. Sally hied away from the table and lumbered across the room to pick up her shotgun while Amos plucked his double barrel from the mantel. He quick footed for the doorway with the others close behind. The four of them spread out on the porch eyeing the horsemen closing from about a quarter of a mile away.

Amos said, 'That's Roy Fisher's palomino. I could spot it anywhere. Bill and Whit are with that bunch too.'

'Karen, you and John come up here,' Jennie called. The two children climbed on to the porch and huddled, half-hidden, behind their mother's skirt.

Horse hoofs shook the ground. Sunlight flashed off Roy Fisher's silver-mounted

151

saddle. Sally counted ten other men; Whit Fisher's roan loped between his sons' horses while the others formed a loose group behind them. They pounded into the yard and drew up before the porch where the Bar F cowboys formed a line before the house.

Whit Fisher's stiff-backed shape fronted his men. His lips drew a straight line across the bottom of his face. A wicked impatience thickened his voice. 'I came for Cliff Leatherwood.'

'I ain't seen hide nor hair of him,' Amos replied.

Rage flickered in the frosty depths of Whit's eyes. One hand closed, opened; he was having a hard time controlling his temper. 'Leatherwood killed one of my men yesterday, and I'm in no mood for talk. Now, trot him out. I mean business.'

'I told you he ain't here.'

Fisher's mouth made a sucking sound. 'Roy, take three men and search that shack.'

As Roy dropped from the palomino, Amos tilted his shotgun waist high. 'This is my house, Fisher. They ain't nobody stepping inside unless I invite them.'

A little shudder ran up Whit's back and the hand on his saddle horn whitened. His Adam's apple slid up and down as splotches colored his flinty cheeks. 'You've got a woman and two kids on that porch. Why don't you use your head?'

Sally's tongue touched the roll of tobacco in her cheek. She knew Amos White was about to explode. Whit Fisher pushed a man too hard. Then she saw some rigidity leave Amos's shoulders as the shotgun tipped downward. Three men dismounted. Sally swallowed tobacco juice when Roy swaggered into the house with the Bar F's hands following. She glanced right, saw the two youngsters gripping their mother's thighs. Jennie's face was the color of moulded hay and her work-reddened hands closed protectively around John and Karen's shoulders. Sally looked back to the front, hearing sludge gurgling in Miles Walker's pipe who stood to the left behind her.

'Bill, take a couple of men and search that barn,' Fisher ordered.

Bill hesitated before he swung out of the saddle and hiked for the barn, two Bar F hands breasting him. Something crashed to the floor inside the house and Amos's huge chest rose with restrained passion. One of the horses shook its head; metal jangled. Voices drifted from the house as a man laughed. Bill's group disappeared into the barn. The horses' fretful snorting was the only sound in that strained silence.

Leather scraped over wood, as Roy and his followers tramped outside and regained their saddles. Miles sidled to the edge of the porch, turned his pipe upside down and knocked dead tobacco into the yard. Whit Fisher lined his angry gaze on Amos as resentment flared in his puritan face.

Roy stuck a cigarette between his pouty lips, lit it, and dropped a hand to his pearl-handled Peacemaker, glaring at Sally. She met Roy's gaze, felt disgust sour her taste buds. Roy was a spoiled brat who needed

154

some manhood slapped into him. His long-barrelled gun, buckskin gloves and leather chaps had him convinced he was one tough sonofabitch. If it wasn't for his last name and that string of riders, someone would have pushed his nose in the dirt years ago.

Bill and his crew returned from the barn. 'Nobody out there,' he said, legging into his saddle.

Whit studied each person on the porch. 'What about it, Miles? Leatherwood over at your place?'

'I've never seen the man.'

Whit's head moved up and down. 'I'm gonna take you at your word, but you people remember this: Leatherwood killed one of my men. I won't stand for that. He has to pay and anybody hiding him has to pay.'

'Maybe he left the country,' Jennie said.

Whit barked a short laugh. 'Not hardly. He thinks he's got a score to settle.' Whit reached into his vest pocket for his pipe, grey eyes dark and bitter. 'What about you,

155

old girl? You're supposed to be his partner. Where's he dug in?'

Sally worked up a mouthful of spittle, spat in the dirt near the roan's feet. 'You bastard. I wouldn't give you the time of day.'

'You better be glad you're a woman. If you weren't, I'd toss a rope over you and drag you around this yard.'

Sally sent another stream of tobacco juice towards the roan. 'Bullshit. You get rid of those bully boys and try to toss a rope around me. You might get the surprise of your miserable life.'

Whit's lids narrowed; the big vein running along the side of his neck pulsed hard and slow. The hand on his saddle horn lost color again. 'I'm about to lose patience with you people. I've tried to be reasonable, but you don't want to be reasonable. Now, I don't want to kill anybody, but I mean to keep what's mine. The best thing you can do is move on, not bring troublemakers in here or side with any who show up. I hear you lost another bunch of sheep last night; I

156

wouldn't advise trying to bring in any more.' With that Fisher whirled his roan and led his crew out of the yard.

Sally spat in the dirt again. 'Dirty sonsabitches. Somebody ought to do something and maybe they will.'

Miles removed the hat from his head, wiped the sweat from his brow. 'I've never seen Whit so worked up. I never figured him for gunplay, but right now I ain't so sure.'

Jennie urged the children toward the yard. 'Karen, you and John go on with your game. Go on now. There's nothing to be afraid of.'

The two children jumped off the porch and disappeared around the corner of the house. A sigh quivered past Jennie's lips. She wiped her hands against the front of her dress while fear and anxiety blunted the angles of her sun-darkened face. 'I still say Rick Pettis is making the right move.'

Amos leaned his shotgun against the wall. Miles stood with his head lowered, nothing showing on the flat surfaces of his hollow cheeks. Sally folded her arms over her breasts. She supported her 150 pounds on straddled legs while her direct, brown eyes stared from beneath the rim of her turned-down hat.

'Just before Fisher rode up, I said I could loan you some money. Are you still interested, or is that sonofabitch scaring you off?'

Amos mumbled something Sally didn't hear. His big hands closed around each other and his blue eyes turned gun-metal blue. 'Whit Fisher don't tell me what to do. How about it, Miles? You sticking?'

Miles's shoulders rose, dropped. A worried expression creased his easy-going face, and he thrust his hands in his hip pockets.

'I don't see that we got any choice. If only Rick and his boys would hang with us.'

'We'll talk to him. He's got to stay.'

Jennie brought a hand to her lips. That far-away expression filled her eyes. She regarded her husband for a long moment, then after glancing from Sally to Miles turned sadly into the house.

Sally rubbed her hands together. She grinned through tobacco-stained teeth. 'God damn! Amos, you rustle all your people over here tomorrow night. I'll get ahold of Cliff. We need to talk this thing over.' Leaving the two men on the porch, she hoofed for the barn. She'd throw a saddle on Nellie and ride into Llano. It made her tingle all over thinking how this was going to nettle that sonofabitch Whit Fisher.

# 11

After his breakfast had been washed down by a third cup of coffee, Leatherwood tramped through the hotel lobby and paused in the shade along the walk. Llano reminded him of a trail town after the cattle season had ended. The place was that dead.

Eventually word would leak out in town, but Fisher wouldn't touch him here. For some reason Fisher felt the need to act like a law-abiding citizen who was reluctantly being forced to defend himself against a bunch of land grabbers.

Leatherwood bowled over the dirt thoroughfare fronting the town's main saloon. He approached the bar, ordered whiskey from the heavy-sideburned bartender. The barkeep put a glass and bottle before him, then moved down to the mahogany's midpoint where he polished some glasses. Leatherwood lit a smoke. He glanced around the room, spotted two townsmen at a rear table and nodded in their direction. The men returned his nod whereupon Leatherwood swung back to the bar and poured two fingers of whiskey.

He had just dropped his cigar butt into a spittoon when hoofbeats drummed down the street. That sound alerted him, drew him to the batwing doors where he saw Sally tie her mule to a hitching rack. As he elbowed outside, his boot heels clicking across the board walk caught Sally's attention. Lowheeled boots scuffing up dust, she ambled up to join him.

She studied his six foot two frame, shook her head despairingly. 'God damn! It didn't take you long to get all prettied up. Last night you looked almost human.'

'Some of us take to dirt better than others. Want a drink?'

'Your suggestion. Your treat.'

He grinned and led the way inside and

signalled for a second glass. 'I guess you've had some company by now.'

Sally wiped the back of her hand over her lips. Her brown eyes sparkled, humour twitching her lips. 'As a matter of fact we did. Seems like you're a popular fellow.'

'Any trouble?'

'Hell, yes. Whit Fisher located that incoming flock of sheep just like you said he would. The sonofabitch run the whole bunch over a cliff. Amos and the others are wiped out.'

'What happens now?'

'Well, they can't eat grass. They've got to get their hands on some money. Bring in some more sheep.'

He shook his head. 'I wish I could help.'

'Seven hundred and fifty dollars would go a long way.'

'You don't give up, do you?'

'Look, Cliff. You know you're going to kill those bastards and the money don't mean a thing to you.'

'That's a fact.'

'So we're finally in this together?'

He nodded, lifted his glass in a toast and swallowed the whiskey. He wanted those men to suffer, but Amos needed the money. He hated breaking his promise to Manuel, but he owed Amos White something, too. Amos had taken him in, fed him, offered him shelter when Amos knew Whit Fisher might use it as a reason to overrun his place.

'How do you think we ought to handle it?' Sally said.

'In the morning we'll head out to Box Canyon. We'll take them or they'll take us.'

'I know a way in there. I think we can take those sonsabitches by surprise.'

Leatherwood refilled the shot glasses. 'To tomorrow.'

Sunlight found them cruising a west-bound road. Sun glistened off dew-encrusted grass; the roadway was damp, holding the dust down. The towering peaks of the Rincon mountains bulked in the distance, and a fresh, morning smell sweetened the air. They followed the road

163

until it bridged the Rincon River. Here the road shot south toward the Bar F while smaller arteries ran in other directions. They left the main thoroughfare following a shallow, well-defined trail pointing toward the mountains. An hour's travel brought them to a waterhole where Bar F cattle grazed in small bunches. Leatherwood spotted horse tracks here, but the sign was blurred and at least three days old.

They cantered south-west, aiming for the big bend that formed an ankle-deep ford three miles from Box Canyon. The sun dried out the grass as its red ball became a yellow blister. Cottonwoods loomed in the distance. A covey of quail flung upward to their right. They rode in silence, each caught in their own thoughts as the cottonwoods edged from a dense mass into individual shapes.

A horseman cantered out of the cotton-woods and, when the distance closed, Leatherwood recognized Sam. The black man spotted them, reined up, then spurred his mustang back toward the trees. Sally's 'I can't keep up', reached Leatherwood as he guided the grey through the trees and into the shallow stretch of river. Water sprayed around him, but he gained on Sam whose startled face stared over one shoulder. Leatherwood drew his revolver, fired a shot that went high as the mustang disappeared behind a ridge of sage. Leatherwood pounded up the stony draw, saw Sam flog up a narrow incline that fed into ravines and jumbled rock.

Trooper clipped up the incline and pounded into an uneven section of land that rose upward. The area was empty. Something tugged at Leatherwood's sleeve as a gunshot boomed from the enclosed heights. Horseshoes clattered to his left, and he burst through a zig-zag turn as Sam urged the mustang into a worm-like aperture that carried him out of sight.

Leatherwood pulled Trooper in, traversed a draw with lifted revolver and a chilled backbone. He didn't know this country and hoped Sam didn't either. The aperture bled into a stretch of grassland funnelling into a dogleg that opened on a rectangular meadow. Across the grassy stretch, the land humped up into rugged canyons that offered innumerable buskwhack locations.

Leatherwood slipped from the grey. If Sam moved, he had to make noise, so the lack of it meant he had dug in waiting for Leatherwood to step into the open and give him another shot. Leatherwood faded back to the grassy draw, followed it south until he found a narrow path leading into the uplands.

He peered around an outcrop of sheltering rock, saw nothing, and dashed across the intervening space to a defile that slanted up to a wall that put him on the second rise in the line of bluffs. He paused by the gnarled branches of a stunted oak, breath hammering around in his lungs while his heart banged his ribcage.

A metallic click sounded above him and a coppery taste soured his mouth. A voice said, 'Drop it.' He debated whether to wheel and fire or take the chance that Sam might not shoot him in the back the moment the revolver fell from his hand. The weight of the derringer dragged at his left arm. If he turned, his only shot would be blind. Better to take the chance that Sam would walk down to him and give him an opportunity to go for the hide-out. The Frontier Colt dropped from his hand to clang against rocky ground. He heard footsteps as pebbles and sand rustled behind him.

Sam said, 'Turn around,' and Leatherwood heeled slowly, hands at his side. The black man stood at less than an arm's length away, a grin revealing wide, white teeth. 'Looks like you finally caught up with me.'

'What are you waiting for?'

'You made me sweat a few days ago. Now, it's your turn.'

Sam's mustang nickered in the background. The sun burned Leatherwood's neck and he knew a quiet desperation. He said, 'Mind if I smoke?' When Sam shrugged, he reached into his vest pocket for a cigar. He fired up and ground the match into the soil. His gaze stayed on the toe of his boot while he steadied the cigar in his teeth with his thumb and forefinger. Then, after four or five long puffs, abruptly he jammed the cigar's red-hot tip into Sam's cheek and swung out to the right with the same motion. Sam screamed. He took an involuntary step backwards as the gun in his hand barked. Before Sam could cock the hammer again, Leatherwood's boot crashed into his hand. Sam's fist flew open, and the force of the kick sent his six-gun flying into the rocks beyond.

Sam groaned as Leatherwood aimed a boot at his belly. Somehow he caught Leatherwood's ankle and toe and, twisting upward, hurled Leatherwood on his back. Leatherwood's head struck a rock. Pain raced down his spine and a redness blurred his vision. He couldn't move, couldn't think, but through a haze he saw Sam push to his feet and stumble toward the mustang.

Leatherwood shook his head violently, tried to clear the surrounding mist as horseshoes clamoured against rock and he realized Sam meant to ride him down. He struggled up to one knee as the mustang bore down on him, and an instant before the horse's shoulder crashed into him, flung himself to the ground.

Instinct told him to move, but he couldn't make his body function. He lay there, his vision a haze of red dashes waiting for the mustang's iron shoes to bash his skull. A sharp, cracking noise pierced the haze, and the ground trembled under a dull drumming. Someone gripped his belt buckle and worked his hips up and down. The red dashes blanketing his vision faded. Sally's competent features appeared above him, and then fresh air filled his windpipe as his greedy lungs sucked in life-giving oxygen.

# 12

Leatherwood sat up. He spat out some blood, ran his tongue around the inside of his busted lips. He sat quite still for a few moments waiting for his head to clear while Sally regarded him with a disgusted expression.

'What do we do now?' Sally asked.

'Damned if I know.'

'We could ride to Box Canyon and take both of them.'

He groaned and closed his eyes. Every inch of his frame ached. 'I'm not sure I could stay in the saddle.'

He heard her boots tap across rock, but was too tired to open his eyes. His head pounded. He heard Sally's returning footsteps; tepid water flushed over his head and dribbled down the sides of his face. The water felt good and he opened his eyes as she recorked the canteen.

'There's a bottle in my saddle-bag. Get it.'

She hiked to Trooper where she fumbled until she found the whiskey. He pulled the cork and took a long swig. The alcohol burned, but a glow formed in his belly and a new vitality sang through him. He took a second pull from the bottle, handed it to her whereupon she tilted the bottle and swallowed about a fourth of its contents.

He rose unsteadily to his feet. Standing slammed fresh pain through him, but he felt stronger now.

'We going after them?'

'Yeah.'

She walked over, picked up his hat and revolver, poked a finger through a hole in the hat's crown. 'You never did tell me about this.'

He placed the hat gently on his head. Then he stepped carefully to where Trooper waited and stirrupped into the saddle. Paroxysms of agony hammered through him as Sally handed him the whiskey bottle which he replaced in his saddle-bag.

She boarded Nellie and led the way into the open country separating the river from the mountain. They followed the foothills south-east. After a while the pounding in his head eased and Trooper's gait over the uneven turf didn't jar him so badly.

They reached the head of the ravine where they paused behind an anvil-shaped boulder. About fifteen yards separated them from the rear of a shack, the back door of which stood open. No air circulated in here. Perspiration gathered across Leatherwood's shoulders and under his hat-band. His throat felt dry, and he wished they'd brought a canteen.

Sally said, 'This place looks deader than a spoiled buffalo.'

Leatherwood nodded as his gaze swept every inch of the canyon. 'Let's hold awhile. We're in no hurry.'

They hid in the boulder's shade for fifteen minutes waiting for something to happen. A hawk's shadow drifted over the land, plunged down at a fieldmouse scurrying for cover. The shadow rose with the mouse's tail drawing a squiggly trail over the baked grass. Leatherwood shifted from one foot to the other. Impatience flared in the middle of his gullet while his normal restraint edged to ill temper. He glanced at his watch, rammed it into his pocket. 'Hell, let's get on with it. Cover me while I move up to the house.'

Sally drew her Peacemaker and used a notch in the rock as a rest for the long barrel while Leatherwood checked his Colt. Then, he dodged across the open ground to the rear of the house where he flattened against the weathered siding. Beyond the open door stood an iron stove, a wood box and a rickety table, but from his position Leatherwood couldn't see all the kitchen, and he could only guess at what occupied the other room. He strained to hear voices, but the only noise was a low, slapping sound he couldn't identify.

173

He waved Sally up and she bounded across the yard. 'What's that noise?'

He shook his head. 'I'm moving in. Keep your eyes open.'

Leatherwood wheeled through the doorway, his gaze rapidly shifting over the room and settling on its single occupant. This man sat behind a makeshift table covered with four rows of cards plus a third of a deck. His chubby hands held a match to the cigar in his teeth. Amazement dilated his black eyes.

A smile broadened his lips as immediately he regained his composure. He dropped the match to the floor and carefully placed both hands on the table. Boots clicked over wood as Sally crossed the kitchen and paused by Leatherwood. Breed's gaze measured her as smoke drifted from his lips. 'Nice to have some company.'

Leatherwood's thumb rested on the 44:40's hammer. Breed's moon face seemed relaxed, confident and nothing showed beneath the black surface of his eyes. Thick black hair, parted in the middle, hung to his shoulders. He appeared completely at ease, but his casual appearance didn't fool Leatherwood.

'Why don't you have some coffee?' Breed said.

'Stand up and unbuckle that gunbelt,' Leatherwood said.

Breed rose to his feet. With his left hand he unbuckled his gunbelt and let it fall to the floor. He removed the cigar from his mouth, expelled smoke as another friendly smile creased his cheeks. 'I know how you feel, but you're making a mistake. I didn't touch that girl. The Fisher brothers are the ones you want.'

'You didn't shoot the old man either?'

'Roy Fisher shot him. Roy had been drinking. He was out of his head. I tried to stop him, but he wouldn't listen.'

Leatherwood fought the rage blinding him. He wanted to smash his gun barrel across Breed's genial face. He wanted to blacken the man's eyes, pound his lips into a bloody pulp. He wanted to disfigure him the way he'd disfigured Carlita. But he was too drained to take Breed head on and something wouldn't let him gun-whip the man to the floor. Maybe he was too proud to let Sally see the hatred overwhelming him. He didn't know what it was, but he couldn't do what he ought to do which was beat this half-breed into a shapeless mass.

'Well, goddamn it, let's get him into town.'

'You bring up the horses.'

Sally gave him a heavy-lidded glance. Her shrewd old eyes flickered over Breed who stood flat-footed and wary.

'Remember, that sonofabitch is worth just as much dead as he is alive.' She rammed her revolver into its holster and clumped over the kitchen and into the yard.

Leatherwood kicked Breed's gunbelt off to one side. Breed puffed casually on his cigar, but his unblinking gaze never left Leather-wood, who felt revulsion thicken his throat, knew that emotion stamped his battered features. Breed had to feel that hatred, had

176

to sense his terrible desire to kill. But Breed only puffed at his cigar, showing no sense of fear if he felt any.

Late afternoon found them trotting down Llano's main street. Two men fronting the mercantile watched them. A horse nickered in the darkened area of the livery's runway. A woman's laugh cackled from the saloon. Two small boys chased a mutt with a tin can tied to its tail into an alley near the bakery.

They reined in at the jail, secured their mounts and escorted Breed into the marshal's office.

Joel Watts sat behind his desk cleaning a rifle. 'Evening.'

Sally said, 'Got a prisoner for you. This sonofabitch is wanted for killing a Wells Fargo driver. The reward's five hundred dollars.'

Joel's lower jaw dropped a full inch. He scratched at his bulging belly. Opening the desk's middle drawer, he pulled out a handful of posters and shuffled through them. He found the one he looked for and laid it on the desk. 'That's him sure enough.' Then he took some keys from the drawer, walked around the desk, and unlocked a cell. 'All right, you; in there.'

'How about the reward money?' Sally asked.

Watts returned to his desk, tossed the keys in the drawer. 'Take a few days. I've got to wire Wells Fargo.'

'Have that draft made out to Sally Bevins. I'll check back with you towards the end of the week.'

# 13

Joel Watts crunched over to the window where he watched Leatherwood and Sally enter the saloon. He pulled at his bulb-like nose, stared thoughtfully into the street before turning back to Breed. 'How in the hell did you get into this spot?'

Breed shrugged. 'Asleep on my feet, I reckon. Now, open this door and let me out of here.'

Joel trudged over to his desk, picked up his keys and clicked the lock. Breed shouldered past him to sink into one of the chairs near the desk.

'They plan to give that money to those sheep herders,' Breed said.

Roy Fisher threw one leg over the saddle horn as he rolled a cigarette. The ground ran lush and green in all directions, its flatness broken only by a few groundswells. This was cattle country with rich grass and plentiful water. About 200 yards to his left, a ring of trees circled a waterhole. Cattle bunched in loose groups and, further out, more Bar F cattle dotted the horizon.

Bill glanced at Roy whose moody expression had bothered him ever since they'd left the ranch. Maybe Roy had had a run-in with the old man. Whit Fisher was a harsh, Old Testament figure at best, hard to please, one who firmly believed in the merits of hard work for himself and those around him. This ranch was his life, and that his sons had different ideas and values upset him. Sometimes he seemed to forget Roy's good points. Roy was courageous, loyal, filled with a lust for life, and completely self-reliant. Whit Fisher demanded respect and obedience, but Roy was slow to give either. He considered his father too old-fashioned, too straight-laced, and too concerned with what others thought. Another facet that caused trouble was despite all his father's efforts, Roy was no cattleman. He was too interested in cards and women to buckle down to the demands of running a ranch. Roy was more concerned with looking like a cattle king than being one.

Roy's gaze shifted to meet Bill's. 'To hell with North Creek. Let's ride into town and have a drink.'

'Pa wouldn't like that.'

'Pa don't have to know.'

'He'll be wanting some answers.'

'And we'll give him some. Quit worrying about what Pa wants. We're old enough to think for ourselves.'

'What's eating you? You've been pouting ever since we left the ranch.'

'Like hell I've been pouting. I've been thinking. The old man's going to keep fooling around until we lose everything. I don't know what's happened to him. I remember the day when he'd have run those sheep herders out in twenty-four hours.'

'You know what Pa says. Things have changed.'

Roy lashed his quirt across his chaps. 'I can think for myself. Did you know that fellow Leatherwood's hanging around Llano and the old man's afraid to go after him?'

'No, I didn't know that.'

'That's the way it is. That bastard came in here looking for trouble and we lack the guts to give it to him.'

Bill's upper lip tucked between his teeth. He stared off into the distance. 'His being here is our fault.'

'Our fault! Hell, *you* didn't do anything. You were about to poo in your pants.'

'I wish to God none of us had done anything.'

Roy's quirt made a loud pop as he slashed it into his left glove. 'The old man and I don't see head to head on most things, but we agree on you: you ain't got enough Fisher blood in you.'

Bill clucked the mare into motion. From the corner of one eye, he saw Roy's palomino trot in stride with the mare. Bill rode without really seeing, letting the mare have its head. One bit of trouble seemed to dovetail into another one, and it had all started when they'd decided to run those sheepmen off. First, that trouble up north had brought Leatherwood. There'd been no cause to murder that old Mexican and to rape his daughter. Both had been grave mistakes.

He rode without seeing; hoofbeats sounded against thick sod and his heart echoed that thumping. What he'd been considering wasn't the end of it. He knew his pa. He was cautious and he would try to run those sheepmen off without personal involvement. But, if not, he'd step in himself. No matter how it happened, the sheepmen would lose out in the end.

Bill rode with head down, thoughts growing gloomier as the miles trickled by. He forgot the time and the place and was surprised when he and Roy approached the main road leading to Llano. Roy's, 'Well, look what we have here', shifted his gaze up the trail where he saw a bulky figure in a flannel shirt and wool hat riding a mule.

Roy reined in the palomino at a position that blocked the trail, and grinned. The woman, who sat astride the mule, spotted them; her shoulders pulled up and, across the distance separating them, Bill sensed the anticipation starching her honest face. He glanced at his brother, saw the malice in his disposition, and alarm tingled the rear of his neck. 'Come on, Roy. Our business is at North Creek.'

'Plenty of time for that. We got more important business right here.'

'Roy, Pa ain't gonna like this.'

'Relax. I don't intend to hurt nobody.'

Sally reined in Nellie just before the mule's nose touched the palomino's. As she switched the reins to her left hand, a wariness narrowed her gaze.

'Where you headed, old girl?' Roy said.

'I don't figure that's any of your goddamned business.'

'You're on Bar F range. That makes it my business. What's your name anyway?'

The old woman spat out a wad of tobacco juice. 'Sally ... Miss Bevins to you.'

'Did you hear that, little brother? Miss Bevins. Now, Miss Bevins, you're trespassing. That could cause you a lot of grief.'

'I don't imagine I've got too much to worry about from the likes of you.'

Colour stabbed up Roy's throat and into his cheeks. He tapped his quirt against his boot. 'You got a smart tongue, Miss Bevins. Maybe I ought to tie a knot in it.'

Bill laid a hand on Roy's arm. 'Come on. We got work to do.'

Roy threw off Bill's hand. His pouty face turned ugly. 'I'll tell you what you're going to do, Miss Bevins. You're turning that mule around and heading back where you came from. In case you've got any items to pick up from the Whites, we'll take you there. Then we'll show you right out of the country. I don't want to see your big-nosed mug around here again. You got that?'

Muscles ridged along Sally's jawline. She dug for the holster at her hip, but before her revolver was half drawn, Roy's Peacemaker covered her.

'Drop it and turn that mule around.'

The pistol fell from Sally's fingers. She put both hands on the reins as if to wheel Nellie around, but instead, she yelled, 'Yi!', kicked Nellie in the ribs, and rammed the mule into Roy's palomino. The horse staggered sideways. When the Peacemaker flipped from Roy's grip, Sally flung herself across the distance. She lined her shoulder into Roy's chest, lifting him from the saddle. They landed on the ground with Sally on top where she slammed a fist into Roy's teeth before he could hurl her aside.

As she tumbled into the grass, Bill leapt from his mare. Roy struggled to his feet and Bill caught his shoulder, whirling him around so that they faced each other. 'Are you crazy? We've caused enough trouble.'

'Keep out of this. I'll kill that old goat.' Roy leapt toward Sally who had crawled to her knees and rammed a down-driving right into her cheek. The blow propelled Sally backward, but before she could fall, Roy grabbed her shirt front and jerked her upright. He slammed a fist into her nose, her mouth, her forehead. At that moment, Bill heard his brother laugh. That laugh sent his 155 pounds into a headfirst flight that ended when his skull crashed into the small of Roy's back. Roy buckled beneath him, and Bill rolled to his feet as Roy shoved up on his haunches.

'That's enough,' Bill said.

Madness still stained Roy's cheeks. His anger was a smell, a hatred, a live thing that pulsed in his gaze. 'When I start something, I finish it. Now get out of the way before you get hurt. You're not big enough to stop me and you know it.'

Bill drew his revolver. The hammer clicked metallically when he thumbed it back. 'I mean it, Roy. Leave her alone.'

'You wouldn't shoot me.'

'I don't want to, but I will. I remember

what you did to that girl. I won't let you leave Sally like you left her.'

Some of the wildness seeped out of Roy's gaze. He wiped a trace of red from his mouth where Sally had hit him. 'I'd say she's learned her lesson. No need in us fighting.'

Bill stepped over to Sally and knelt beside her.

'She's hurt bad, Roy. She needs a doctor.'

'Somebody will find her.'

'I'm headed for Amos White's place. He's got a wagon. We can get her into town.'

# 14

Leatherwood glanced in the mirror to see Amos White approach the bar. Leatherwood signalled the bartender for a glass. 'Amos, you've got trouble written all over you.'

'I just left Sally at the doctor's.'

Leatherwood downed his own drink. 'What happened?'

'Roy Fisher beat hell out of her. Got a couple of fractured ribs. I guess she was lucky at that.'

Leatherwood studied his glass, thoughts tumbling backwards.

'That fellow's sure hell on women.' He filled his glass feeling rage knuckle the big muscles across the top of his shoulders. He looked at Amos's lowered head. The man's neck was so thick that there seemed to be no junction between his head and his body.

Grabbing the bottle, Amos poured himself a drink. 'First Tom, now Sally. I'm gonna have to kill that sonofabitch.'

The whiskey burned Leatherwood's throat. He put the glass on the bar, placed a hand on Amos's bicep. It felt like iron. The man was that solid.

'Forget it. You've got a wife and two kids to consider.'

'It don't matter. What happened to Sally and Tom happened because of me.'

'I'll take care of the Fishers. That's why I'm here.'

'I owe them something, too.'

'I know how you feel, but let me handle it. I've got some more bad news. Breed's out of jail. My guess is if we stash him there fifty times, he'll *escape* fifty times. Sally won't collect any reward on Breed or Sam. Not in this town.'

'Then I guess we're finished.'

'You and your family were nice to me. I want to pay you back, so I intend to finish this business.'

'You're going after Roy?'

'I'll take Breed and Sam first, then the Fisher boys.'

Amos scrubbed a hand across his cheek. He had the kind of skin that would never tan, that would always look sunburned.

'I feel sorry for Bill. He's not a bad kid. He tried to help Sally.'

Leatherwood's steel gaze shifted off to the left. 'Maybe he's learned something, but he learned too late.'

After Amos departed, Leatherwood poured another drink. He should have helped Amos, but he didn't want to see Sally's battered face. This was a time for a cool head, not madness.

The batwing doors creaked and boots pounded over the rough flooring. Leatherwood felt the bar give as someone leaned his weight against it, but his mind stayed on Sally. A voice yelped, 'Give me a beer', a voice that sent shock travelling down Leatherwood's back. He straightened, glanced to his left and saw Roy Fisher.

Lifting his beer, Roy spun so that he faced Leatherwood. 'Here's to those four-flushers who think they can move in on Bar F grass.'

Along the bar, men ducked their heads. At the one occupied table, four poker players froze in rigid attention while the barkeep edged away from the bar. Leatherwood heard the challenge in those words, saw it in the way Roy swallowed his beer and slammed down his empty stein. A tic tingled the corner of Leatherwood's mouth. Bitterness filled his throat. Adrenalin pumped into his veins – pushing him, pushing him.

Roy snickered. 'Boys, meet Mr Leatherwood. He rode all the way down here to find the folks who killed his best friend. Now if what was done to his friend was done to mine, I'd be making things even. Not staring down into a whiskey glass.'

A shudder tore from the top of Leatherwood's head to the sole of his boots. Blood pumped against the insides of his skull and his jaw hurt. He pushed away from the bar and, as he stepped toward the door, Roy swaggered in front of him. 'You're wearing a gun; ain't you got the guts to use it?'

Leatherwood swallowed the bile in his throat. Heat flushed his body. The only thing in his world was Roy's sneering face. He slammed a right into that face which drove Roy into an empty table that tipped under his weight and flipped him to the floor.

As Leatherwood moved back, a deep flush colored Roy's face. He sprang to his feet and, with pumping fists, swirled forward. Leatherwood blocked those blows with his arms and shoulders. He clipped Roy in the mouth, the nose, the temple. Blood trickled from Roy's nostrils; his lips puffed up. He swung wildly at Leatherwood's chin, but Leatherwood ducked, jabbed another hard left into Roy's nose and the trickle turned into a surge of crimson that covered Roy's upper lip.

He battered Roy's mouth and nose with sharp, stinging punches. Swinging wildly, Roy surged forward, but Leatherwood deflected his fists. Laughter bubbled in his throat. He planted a right in Roy's mid-section that drove the wind from his half-open mouth. The blow changed Roy's complexion to a sallow grey and, gasping for air, he fell to one knee.

Leatherwood stood over him. The arrogance had left Roy's face; all the cockiness had been beaten out of him. His ballooned-up mouth trembled in a desperate grimace. Leatherwood saw fear in those once proud eyes. He'd never been a brutal man, but he suddenly knew he would pound Roy's paled countenance until it resembled one he couldn't forget. A voice he didn't recognize snarled, 'Get up. This has just begun.'

Roy shook his head. 'I've had enough.'

'Get up before I kick your teeth out.'

Roy's Adam's apple bobbed frantically. His gaze jumped around the room, but the onlookers avoided it. In the background someone coughed and a man nervously cleared his throat.

The barkeep eased around the mahogany.

'He's had enough.'

The look on Leatherwood's face sent the bartender back behind the counter. Leatherwood kicked Roy in the shins, saw the fear in Roy's eyes turn to terror. The expression lit a fire in Leatherwood's belly. His hand closed around Roy's shirt front and he hauled Roy's 210 pounds of quaking flesh upright. A muffled groan shuddered through his broken mouth. He attempted to bring his hands up to protect his face, but Leatherwood banged a fist through that flabby defence that landed on Roy's cheek. He hit him in the eyes, the nose and the mouth until Roy's moans became low, unintelligible, sobs.

Then something hard and round pressed into the small of Leatherwood's back. A voice said, 'Let him go before you kill him.'

Leatherwood's fist paused in mid-air. The metal pressed harder against his spine. When the pressure on his back released, he heeled around to find Marshal Joel Watts eyeing him.

Watts kept his pistol pointed at Leatherwood. 'Some of you men carry Roy over to the doc's office. You'd better come with me.'

'I didn't start it. He did.'

A grey-headed townsman nodded. 'He's right, Joel. Roy wouldn't let him alone.'

Reluctantly, Watts bolstered his revolver. 'I've had all the trouble from you I want. If you've got any brains, you'll leave this country while you're able to leave.'

As two townspeople lugged Roy Fisher outside, Leatherwood watched the marshal's departing back. He glanced down at his bloodstained knuckles and a sense of satisfaction flooded him. As he'd figured, it hadn't been much of a fight. Roy had cowed people because of the Bar F. In his entire life, probably no one had dared stand up to him because of his old man.

'Where the hell have you been?' Whit demanded.

Roy swung wearily from the palomino. His

196

broken nose throbbed, his puffed eyes ached, the bruises on his face burned and his swollen lips made it difficult to answer.

'I've been to town, Pa.'

'I told you to keep out of Llano. And another thing: I told you Breed and Sam would take care of that woman. Now, don't blame your brother. I wrung it out of him. I knew something was wrong when you two didn't come back together.'

Lamplight pencilled a thin line through the doorway. It yellowed the toes of Roy's boots. He fought to keep his voice natural. This had to be done right or he was in for more hell. 'I'm sorry about what happened, Pa. It was an accident. That old gal kept pushing me. She wouldn't let up.'

'Yeah. Like those friends of Leatherwood pushed you. Now what in the hell were you doing in Llano?'

'I knew Bill was helping Amos White get that old girl into town. I was looking for Amos.'

Whit slammed a boot against the floor,

snorted. A rocker squeaked. Roy shifted his weight from his left leg to his right.

'What did you want with Amos?'

'I found ten head of stock with their heads blown off.'

This time Whit did push out of the chair. 'You found ten head of dead beef!'

'You heard me. I figured it had to be Amos. You never see him without that shotgun. I told you we ought to run those squatters off. If we don't do something, they're gonna kill our beef like we did their mutton.'

A strangled voice lifted from Whit's position. His ramrod shape formed a solid weight in the dim light. 'All right, you looked for him. Did you find him?'

'I found Leatherwood instead.'

'And you're still walking? Maybe he's not as tough as I thought.'

Roy took two steps that put him in the lamplight. 'He's tougher than I thought he was.'

A strangled noise escaped Whit's throat.

Bill's, 'Good God!' funnelled in from the left. Whit studied Roy's pulpy face and a different anger tempered his voice. 'Let's get inside. I want to get a better look at you.'

They pushed into the living-room where Whit's lips slimmed as rage flushed his cheeks. 'I'll kill him for this. Plus ten dead head of beef. Those people must be crazy.'

'We don't know it was Amos,' Bill said. 'Nobody saw him.'

Roy's head lifted as scorn loaded his voice. 'You know Amos blames us for Tom's death. Who else could it have been? Damn it, Pa. We've got to move against those people.'

Whit grunted, 'You're right, Roy. Been right all along. I made a mistake waiting for those folks to go broke. Maybe I am getting too old to handle things. Maybe I ought to turn more of the responsibility over to you. If I had, this trouble would have been over. Bill, I want you on the trail by sun-up. Bring in every hand we got to the ranch by noon. We're going skunk hunting.'

Bill licked a paper, folded it over tobacco

and stuck it in his mouth. 'Pa, we don't have to do it this way. Those folks are strapped. If Leatherwood doesn't come up with that money, they're finished. All you have to do is pay off Breed and Sam. We don't need them any more.'

'You're right. We don't need them. They're trash. It's time we did our own fighting.'

'Why fight? Without the money, Amos and the rest will have to leave. We ride in on him tomorrow, somebody's liable to get killed.'

A sneer jerked at Roy's busted mouth. 'At best we'll find four or five individuals at any of those sheep digs. They ain't gonna fight twenty armed men.'

'What if something goes wrong? Somebody loses their head?'

'That ain't our fault.'

'Pa, I still think...'

Whit's hand viciously chopped the air. 'I don't want to hear any more. Ever since that bunch has been here you've wanted to turn that section over to them. That's Fisher land. Always was, always will be. You round-up those men like I told you. And no more back talk.'

The flush of success formed a glow on Roy's battered face.

# 15

Dawn fell into the canyon like a curtain of light rain. The two-room shack formed a dull blot twenty yards out from Leatherwood's position. There was no sign of life.

Leatherwood slithered across the intervening distance. He heard nothing, saw nothing except the oblong-shaped outhouse off to the left. As he reached the cabin's back door, the first pink glow of sunlight shimmered off the canyon's east wall. He paused, listened intently, then tried the door. It opened before his touch and, revolver in hand, he crept into the kitchen. It was darker in here, but he made out the dim outline of a table, three chairs and a wood stove.

He glided past the stove, reached the connecting room and glanced over it. What appeared to be a bedroll lay against the left wall and, directly across from it, he saw a shadowy space that looked like a second bedroll. As a snore shuddered from the left bedroll, Leatherwood slipped to the table, removed the lamp's globe, lit the wick and replaced the globe as light flickered over the room.

Leatherwood eared back the hammer of his .44:40. He kicked over one of the chairs and it rattled across the floor. The noise jerked up Breed. When his sleep-puffed gaze located Leatherwood, stunned expression slackened his moon countenance; then, his full lips parted into a grin.

Something cold and round and hard pressed against the back of Leatherwood's head. Sam said, 'Put your pistol on the table.'

Acid dripped into Leatherwood's stomach. A tart taste flooded his throat. The gun pressed harder against his skull, but he kept his Colt's muzzle on Breed who shoved to his feet.

'You'd better drop it,' Breed said.

'There's a hair trigger on this gun. Even if he blows my head off, my reflexes will kill you.'

Breed's grin widened. 'Nobody's talking about killing.'

'Then tell your partner to put his gun down.'

A chuckle slid past Breed's lips. 'How'd he miss you, Sam?'

'I've had the skitters all night. Saw him just as I started to leave the outhouse.'

'Lucky for us. Now, look. We came here to do a job and it's done. We're ready to ride out. Those Fisher boys are the ones you want. If it hadn't been for them, there wouldn't have been no trouble. I under-stand how you feel, but we can both win. You get the Fishers; we go back where we came from.'

It was cool in the room, but sweat formed under Leatherwood's shirt. Breed's hands lifted in a supplicating gesture, but his black-button eyes reflected none of the amiability of his face. His grin was forced, his cheeks a mask, for brutality pulsed beneath his surface posture.

Leatherwood shrugged; his chin dipped and he saw a subtle change in Breed's expression. As Breed stepped forward, Leatherwood lifted his left arm so that his hand was heart high. He dropped the .44:40 and the pistol hit the floor with a force that jarred the hammer loose and sank the firing pin into the cartridge. At the unexpected explosion, Cliff Leatherwood felt the pressure of Sam's gun relax. As the startled man jerked backwards, Leatherwood's right hand dove into his open sleeve. As the derringer pulled free, he whirled and fired a slug into Sam's incredulous face. The slug tunnelled a red hole between the black man's eyes. Leatherwood's whirl brought him around full circle in time to see Breed wheel toward the blankets.

'You'll never make it,' he said, and Breed halted as knowledge shoved his round countenance out of shape.

Breed grinned again, white, wide-spaced teeth showing, 'Looks like it's your play.'

Light poked through the windows, over-shadowing the lamp's glow. Leatherwood dropped to one knee and scooped up the Colt. He thrust the derringer in his belt, transferred the revolver to his right hand and pointed it at the 'breed's mid-section. Two shots rocked the room as he clutched his stomach and sank to the floor. Leatherwood hiked over to him, stared down into those black-button eyes.

'I promised Manuel I'd make it last, so you'll have to hurt enough for two people.'

# 16

From a point halfway between the Rincon River and the second range of hills surging into the mountains Sally Bevins heard a volley of pistol shots, and her gaze caught Leatherwood's hard-running grey disappear into an open draw before a group of riders raced into the open space fronting it. She counted five men in the bunch which brought a grin to her homely face. She'd been right in assuming Whit would split up his outfit. This band at the mountain's north reaches meant that a second group closed from the south, with at least one other crew bunched somewhere in between. The unknown horsemen were the ones she had to worry about. The men after Cliff wouldn't notice her until she rode through them; then it would be too late, for she would have the advantage, but that same advantage belonged to the fellows she couldn't place.

She glanced at the men accompanying her. Gay Walker's teeth flashed whitely while a satisfied expression bunched his long jaw. Gay enjoyed this; he was still young. Too young to comprehend what could happen. Rick Pettis knew. His suddenly aged visage reflected the fear and anxiety that kept him hump-shouldered and thin-lipped. Al breasted his dad; lean, dark countenance ridged and unsure. He wasn't petrified like his father, but he didn't share Gay's enthusiasm. Will brought up the rear. His complacent features looked tough for once. He didn't like this, but he'd committed himself and showed a backbone that Sally hadn't expected.

The four of them saw what she saw, so, when she kicked Nellie in the flanks, they didn't fall behind. Abruptly, she wished she'd ridden a horse. Nellie was dependable, but speed she lacked. More gunshots rippled down to her as the Bar F hands entered the draw. The land turned stony under Nellie's hoofs while the land tilted, became a series of ravines and gullies and canyons. Sally's cracked ribs ached, causing her to suck harder on the plug of Twist tucked in her gum. She'd never endured so much pain; but if she could just get the sonofabitch Roy Fisher in her sights, the misery would be worth it.

They reached the small end of the funnel-shaped draw. Up ahead grew two clumps of timber separated by a length of meadow-land. She recognized Roy's palomino leading a Bar F crew in from the southeast. Roy's crew met the bunch chasing Cliff, and someone pointed into a stand of timber off to the left. Roy shouted something, waved west and, as the first Bar F group spurred toward the meadow, Roy urged his men into the woodland.

The Bar F had Cliff trapped in there. The bunch she followed raced to seal him off while Roy and the others dogged him like beaters flushing game. She couldn't take her people into those pines. Hell, they might shoot each other or Cliff, but they could circle through that meadowland after the others, come up on them, and smash the ambush.

The pines stood fifty yards out and she noted that the woods were thick with undergrowth. A shot rang out. Somebody screamed. The taste of dust, sweat and excitement made her forget her ribs as she thundered around the woodlands with the others clattering behind.

Sally drew her Peacemaker. Gay levelled his handgun while the others rode with rifles at the ready. A stubby thumb of pines jutted into the meadow. Sally's band rounded that thumb to come up on the Bar F riders who formed a half-circle facing the woodland.

The Pettis boys pulled up at some boulders. They rolled into shelter and returned the Bar F fire. As Rick reached his sons, he fell out of the saddle and flopped over on his belly. Sally reined Nellie in by Rick's horse and flung herself off the mule. The impact of her boots meeting the ground sent red spots dancing before her as pain from the cracked ribs hammered through her.

Al glanced their way. When he spotted his father his complexion turned the color of dirty wash water. Al humped back and, with Sally's help, dragged Rick in behind the rocks. Al said, 'Is he dead?'

Sally nodded. She ignored the lead glancing off rock and put a comforting hand on Al's shoulder.

'Jesus! What are we gonna tell Ma?' Will mumbled.

'He died like a man. He wasn't afraid.'

'But he didn't want to come. Good God a'mighty! He didn't want any part of this.'

'I know, but either we finish it or those sonsabitches do.'

Leatherwood came to a stop. In these trees and dense underbrush, he'd lost all sense of direction and wondered if he had walked in some kind of a circle. He didn't dare mark a trail for to do so would lead his pursuers right to him. Sweat stung his armpits. A broken branch had ripped a hole in his shirt. He felt dirty and his body odor smelled as rank as the mouldy leaves he stumbled over.

He pressed through shoulder-high brush. The pines were wide spaced here with thicker trunks. It seemed to thin out ahead, and he had a hunch he was about to reach open ground. He could see the sun now, but he still couldn't get his bearings. The ground seemed to pitch off to the left which could mean it pitched to the east toward the river.

'Don't move and don't turn around.'

These words rammed into Leatherwood's brain like a blunt axe. A sick thrill coursed up his spine while a tinny taste filled his throat again.

'Drop your gun and walk about six-eight yards from your horse. Then turn around.'

The Colt fell from his fingers; it thudded against the dirt. With all that tin making it hard to swallow, Leatherwood moved out eight big steps and heeled around.

Roy edged from behind a clump of juniper. 'You've given me a hell of a time. Was it worth it?'

'It would be if I could have finished it.'

'You got halfway.'

'Not the half I wanted.'

'You damn fool. You actually thought you could touch me? This is Bar F country.'

'You only up to killing old men and raping young women? What are you waiting for? A crowd to show off in front of?'

'You think you're a pretty hard customer, don't you? Before this is over, you'll beg me to kill you.'

Leatherwood stuck a cigar in his teeth, chewed on it. His gaze flicked beyond Roy, reached Trooper's long nose, velvet nostrils. Roy stood directly in front of the gelding with not over four feet separating them. He glanced back to Roy, read the wild look in

Roy's expression.

Roy bit out some words. 'I'll fill you so full of holes you'll sag like a pair of old springs.'

Leatherwood removed the cigar from his mouth. His lips sucked in and a piercing whistle blasted through his teeth.

Trooper's ears perked. His long legs churned as he lunged forward.

Roy heard those hoofbeats. His mouth fell open as he threw a glance at the hard-driving gelding and tried to hurl himself from Trooper's path. The grey brushed Roy's shoulder and, while Roy desperately struggled to maintain his balance, Leatherwood dove for his six-shooter. His hand closed around the wooden grips, he levelled the sights on Roy's fear-maddened face and squeezed the trigger. Roy's forehead became a blood-splattered mass. The gunshot rocketed over space and the stinging taste of gun powder percolated into Leatherwood's mouth.

# 17

The bowl-shaped basin emptied into a line of flat-topped hills splashed with pine and oak. Amos White directed his followers across that basin and at a slow trot worked his way through a series of gullies and washes. From higher up, gunshots sent warped echoes bouncing across the gullies. Tobacco juice dribbled down Amos's chin as his strong teeth flayed a chunk of Twist. He couldn't tell exactly where the shooting originated and it bothered him, because the location would tell him whether it was Cliff or Sally trapped in the shoot-out.

'I hope that ain't Sally and the others,' Kyle muttered.

'So do I. If they've spotted her, they'll be expecting the rest of us.'

Dallas's stallion breasted Amos's piebald

where Dallas glared at him. 'There's fighting up there.'

'All right!' Amos eyeballed Dallas then spurred through a stony pass with the others bunched behind him. They thundered out of the pass into an open plateau that extended toward a clump of timber half hidden by a wall of rock. A single shot boomed and fainter pistol fire cracked erratically from behind a clump of hills several hundred yards beyond the woodland.

Horse hoofs clattered to the rear, swinging Amos around to where seven riders rammed on to the plateau from a canyon off to the left. Whit Fisher led the pack while Bill's mare ran neck and neck with his father's roan. Further ahead, Amos saw Leatherwood flog out of the timber and his heart missed a beat as he realized that they were caught between Whit's outfit and the Bar F chasing Leatherwood.

More gunshots zipped around them. Dallas screamed, 'My leg! My leg!' and Kyle and Tucker Cline sent rifle fire toward the onrushing riders. 'Let's get into those rocks,' Amos yelled. He kicked the piebald into action just as four Bar F burst from the trees throwing bullets at the hard-riding Leatherwood.

Amos's band scrambled for cover. They rested their rifles on some rocks and hurled a volley of lead into the Bar F crew who rushed into the hills that formed a backdrop to the south.

Leatherwood steered Trooper into the boulders shielding Amos and the others. He almost fell out of the saddle and crawled up to where Amos knelt behind a wall of granite. 'We can't just sit here,' he said.

'Why not?' Tucker asked.

'Because Whit will have his crew into higher land. Once they find the right angle, we'll have about as much chance as a wounded duck.'

'What are we going to do?' Amos mumbled.

'We'll have to move. Hit Whit before he can dig in.'

Leatherwood saw Tucker and Miles exchange hooded glances as concern puckered Kyle's prunelike visage. Leatherwood shoved to his feet noting that Amos rose with him. He had to get this bunch going before their doubts solidified and they made up their minds not to leave the safety of these rocks. He handed his Winchester to Dallas. 'Try to keep those boys pinned down.'

'What about my leg?' Dallas groaned.

'You don't need a leg to shoot a rifle. Now, start pouring some lead into that bunch. Give us some cover.'

As rifle bullets peppered the uphill stakeouts, Leatherwood swung on Trooper and pounded into the flats with the others following. They galloped over the plateau with only five or six shots blasting around them before reining in behind an outcrop.

Leatherwood glanced down into the country they had ridden through. He could see the boulders where Dallas was dug in, but he lacked the angle to see him. He spotted his horse while, off to the right, the checkered shirts of Fisher's men made tiny splotches of color behind the boulders they used for shelter.

A narrow ledge wound around a cliff, disappeared, then reappeared to climb higher up another stony path. Leatherwood waved his crew on, and the horses plodded along the ledge weaving in and out of steep hillocks.

The ledge opened on to a stretch of broken rock that bucked into a growth of evergreens walling off the area beyond. Rifle fire sounded louder here and Leatherwood suspected this band of timber choked the ground reaching the ridge or overhang utilized by Whit Fisher. The woods couldn't be too deep otherwise the firing would be muffled.

'Amos, leave your horse here and see if you can locate Fisher. He's up there behind those trees.'

His cigar was only a quarter smoked when Amos stepped from the saplings and puffed up to him. 'There's seven of them up there on a ridge. It's about a five-minute walk. These woods are pretty thin. I don't think we ought to ride in.'

Whit's men ceased firing and Leatherwood inched toward the ridge. A wrong move, a sudden noise would alert them, and a shoot-out would follow that he wanted to avoid. If they could get the drop on Fisher's crew, the thing was finished. He reached the edge of the timber and eased on to the ridge as a sharp, popping sound shattered the stillness. Leatherwood watched Whit Fisher whirl around, saw the rancher's strict features crook in disbelief. Whit flung up his revolver and triggered a desperate shot just as Leatherwood's slug smashed into his chest and knocked him backwards.

From where he settled behind a knotted pine trunk, Leatherwood had a clear view. Whit lay sprawled and, an arm's length from him, a blue-shirted cowboy lay crumpled. Leatherwood heard a gasp followed by Tucker's, 'Oh, my God'. Then he spotted

Kyle's white-haired form lying face down.

A rifle barrel with a handkerchief tied to it poked over the gully.

'Can we talk?'

Leatherwood glanced at the others. That was Bill Fisher's voice. 'Why not?'

'My father's dead. I think I can talk my brother into settling this peacefully. There's been enough killing.'

'Your brother's dead.'

'You killed Roy?'

'That's right, which leaves only you.'

'The problem is between you and me. No need in anybody else getting killed. We're coming out.'

Hands over his head, Bill walked from the gully with the five Bar F hands filing behind. They halted on the middle of the ledge and dropped their gunbelts.

Bill stared off into nothing. 'Let's get down to those rocks. I'll call my people out.'

Leatherwood nodded as a strange, hollow sensation swelled up in his chest. Damn if he didn't feel sorry for Bill Fisher and he didn't want to feel sorry. The man owed him something he intended to collect. Gunfire scattered below. He would handle Bill later. Right now a more pressing problem needed solving.

Staggered gunshots ripped the air as the Bar F men drew in behind a rounded slope separating them from the plateau. Bill cupped his hands to his lips. 'Listen, you men. This is Bill Fisher. Drop your guns and come out.' With that, Bill clucked his mare into the open and waited for the Bar F crew to reach him.

Amos's broad frame was lax with relief. Bill swung the mare around so that he faced Leatherwood, but his gaze flickered to one side. Leatherwood considered the emotion shaping Bill Fisher's face.

A flurry of gunfire crackled northward. 'I'd better stop this,' Bill said.

Strain touched Leatherwood's jaw. He felt hollow again. Bill sucked his lips into his mouth. 'I know what you're thinking, but I won't run. I give you my word. I didn't touch your friends.'

'You were there. You didn't try to stop it.'

The sound of four quick shots waffled down to them. Bill's clenched teeth showed as despair puffed out his cheeks. 'I was afraid, but you wouldn't understand that. Please. Let me stop what's going on up there. I won't run.'

Leatherwood studied the blue eyes of the young man directly fronting him. Bill looked older than he had back on the ridge and his skin was a corpse's waxy grey. Leatherwood nodded. 'If you say you didn't touch them, I believe you. You'd best get into those hills before someone else gets hurt.'

Leatherwood stuck a cigar between his teeth, blew out a long streamer of smoke. A few days' rest would make him a new man, then he would ride out of here. The reward for Breed and Sam would get Amos and the others started, and he could pick up his life where it had ended that day at Manuel's Corazon ranch.

This Large Print Book for the partially
sighted, who cannot read normal print, is
published under the auspices of
**THE ULVERSCROFT FOUNDATION**

## THE ULVERSCROFT FOUNDATION

... we hope that you have enjoyed this
Large Print Book. Please think for a
moment about those people who have
worse eyesight problems than you ... and
are unable to even read or enjoy Large
Print, without great difficulty.

You can help them by sending a
donation, large or small to:

**The Ulverscroft Foundation,
1, The Green, Bradgate Road,
Anstey, Leicestershire, LE7 7FU,
England.**
or request a copy of our brochure for
more details.

The Foundation will use all your help to
assist those people who are handicapped
by various sight problems and need
special attention.

Thank you very much for your help.